From Tails to Tales

From Tails to Tales

Discovering philosophical treasures in picture books

Maria daVenza Tillmanns

IGUANA

Publisher: Cheryl Hawley
Editor: Holly Warren
Cover image: Roger Gutierrez
Illustrations for Why We Are in Need of Tails: Blair Thornley
All other Illustrations: Students of El Toyon Elementary School in
San Diego, with parental permission, credited separately below each
illustration

ISBN 978-1-77180-665-7 (hardcover)
ISBN 978-1-77180-666-4 (paperback)
ISBN 978-1-77180-664-0 (epub)

This is an original print edition of *From Tails to Tales*.

This book constitutes a loving plea for practicing philosophy with children and adults alike, to get a closer connection with each other, a deeper understanding. To reconnect to each other and to this beautiful world we live in. In a lighthearted way it explains complex philosophical notions so they become understandable to elementary school children.

—Claartje van Sijl, PhD, coach and philosophical counselor
for academics

So, what is this book about? How did its author manage to put big philosophy into a small story? It is written in dialogue, so the reader immediately plunges into a lively conversation. Dialogue not only sharpens attention, but also invites the reader to participate in the conversation. The stories Huk and Tuk discuss, though simple in content, are deep in meaning. DaVenza Tillmanns manages to reflect the main existential questions that sooner or later arise in each of us. These questions address issues of everyday life, loneliness, authenticity, the integrity of the individual, life and death. And essentially, all are contingent on how we make our decisions in life.

—Sergey Borisov, Doctor of Philosophy, Professor, Head of the
Department of Philosophy and Cultural Studies of the South Ural State
Humanitarian Pedagogical University (Chelyabinsk, Russia), President of
the Association of Philosophers Practitioners "Ratio"

I have experienced Maria's lessons in the past. The way she gets students to think and her questioning are definitely creating higher-level thinkers. I want to be able to do the same. If we can get children to be thinkers and to view topics from different points of view, they can apply this thinking in all areas at school and in life. It has forced me to reflect on my own thinking.

—Patricia Carrillo, classroom teacher and English learner site liaison, El Toyon Elementary School, National City, California

I think Ms. Maria makes us think deeper by asking us questions we usually wouldn't think to ask ourselves. I really enjoy listening to all the stories read to us by Ms. Maria. After each story, Ms. Dang and Ms. Maria would ask us questions and we would answer and discuss our different ideas and offer questions of our own.

—Mustafa Al Wiswasee, third grade student, 2017, El Toyon Elementary School, National City, California

To the Seventh Generation

Contents

Picture Books Huk and Tuk Discuss

You can imagine the ridiculousness of an art historian taking his students to museums, having them write a thesis on some historical or technical aspect of what they see there, and after a few years of this giving them degrees that say they are accomplished artists. They've never held a brush or a mallet and chisel in their hands. All they know is art history.

Yet, ridiculous as it sounds, that is exactly what happens in the philosophology that calls itself philosophy. Students aren't expected to philosophize. Their instructors would hardly know what to say if they did. They'd probably compare the student's writing to Mill or Kant or somebody like that, find the student's work grossly inferior and tell them to abandon it.

—Robert S. Pirsig

Foreword

So many are quick to underestimate children's stories, relegating them to juvenile libraries and missing the enormity of scope and potential benefit for readers of any age.

As with a timeless song, a listener is uniquely impacted through exposure to one of these stories depending on their circumstances in that precise moment. Similarly, many of these well-loved stories also stand the test of time, not only across generations of children, but also across readers and listeners of all ages.

Maria daVenza Tillmanns elevates these stories by weaving in the explicit contemplation of Huk and Tuk. Through their lens, readers are offered new ways to consider the embedded narrative and may even assign enriched meaning to their own lives. While Huk and Tuk shine a light on different aspects of each tale, make no mistake as to who their puppeteer is. This expert teacher guides the willing reader to realizations that they likely never saw coming. Through their dialogue, these characters model perspective, confirmation and extension of ideas, and demonstrate how to go further in tandem, exploring more deeply than one may have ventured alone. As daVenza Tillmanns explains, "Huk is not Tuk and Tuk is not Huk. They are Huk and Tuk." And the reader is neither Huk nor Tuk. Yet, through this interaction, we learn. DaVenza Tillmanns masterfully shows up, through Huk and Tuk, in how she gently encourages us and beckons us to actively think and question.

Viewing the beloved children's stories from this new philosophical vantage point, Huk and Tuk feel like familiar characters, fitting well within the universe of children's literature. As such, the reader doesn't necessarily recognize which is the familiar and which is the novel in this framework. The reader is led along this contemplative path willingly, delightfully, holding on to each word, tasting it fully, and once moved forward, they cannot unthink. There is no going back to unknowing.

Still, every time the reader has the opportunity to pick up this book again, they are on a new journey with the same words. It is only the reader in this precise moment who is different.

We may have already read or heard one or more of the stories Huk and Tuk discuss, but never with this treatment and never at this point in our lives.

We are not only enriched by the content based on our context, we are transformed by how Huk and Tuk model the inquiry and interpretation of ideas and, through their dialogical exploration, we may formulate our own perspectives. We can explore vicariously through the characters' actions so that we may benefit, almost as if their learning history is our own.

This is the gift that daVenza Tillmanns bestows upon her students, young and old — the core of what makes us human — how to think, how to independently consider an idea, a story, a text, another person's viewpoint, and how to navigate its impact.

We are now keepers of these stories and our new ways of thinking. And that is not by luck, but by virtue of being in the hands of a master philosopher, a true educator.

Brava.

—Becca Yuré

Preface

My journey into the world of philosophy started as a high school student in the Netherlands, where Ancient Greek and Latin were required courses for six years. I found that the Greeks particularly had great insight into the human condition, and they fascinated me. By the time I headed off to university, I had developed a keen interest in ancient philosophy, especially Plato, and existentialism.

When it came to dealing with the human condition, philosophy as an art form has always seemed more powerful to me than philosophy as a theory (or a multitude of theories). Yet most philosophers are academics rather than artists. After receiving my bachelor of arts in philosophy from Clark University in 1978, I attended a summer workshop by Dr. Matthew Lipman, the founder and director of the Institute for the Advancement of Philosophy for Children at Montclair State University. I found this form of doing philosophy — rather than just teaching its history — very inspiring.

Over the years, I worked as a philosopher-in-residence at various elementary schools, libraries and churches in the United States and the Netherlands, and I found that what brought me closest to the art of philosophy was working with children. I found my niche when practicing philosophy with children because children wonder about their surroundings and have an intuitive understanding of the world. They have their own ideas or insights about, for example, what fairness entails or what true friendship is. When children ask questions, adults often mistakenly think that they are looking for answers, but that's not exactly it — really, it's their endless curiosity that's driving their persistent questioning. Questions also invite us (the adults) to engage with them. That, I believe, is what children want most of all. Answers in themselves never seem quite good enough for them.

As a university lecturer, I always told my students that knowledge cannot replace thinking. With an ever-increasing emphasis on knowledge-based learning, learning for the sake of developing one's own thinking often falls by the wayside. Students may acquire great knowledge from their academic studies, but do they really gain a deeper understanding of what they learn? Instead of learning the answers for things, are they able to ask the next meaningful question?

After leaving the academy, I immersed myself in doing philosophy with children full time. I was philosopher-in-residence at a private school and later at an underserved school in San Diego. Reading picture books with elementary school students and discussing these stories with them inspired me to write the Huk and Tuk series.

The stories in this series are whimsical and playful, with ideas that emerged from the picture books the students, their teachers and I read and discussed during my residency. The main characters, Huk and Tuk, tell stories from these picture books and wrestle, juggle and play with the questions that come up as a result, questions like Is something ever truly

Fairy Tails

Once upon a time, before we had fairy tales, we had
actual tails. Everyone had them.

Everyone had them.

It made sense. Tails connected us to the world and to others and wove us into the fabric of life.

We had long tails, which we would drape over our arms, casually throw around our necks like scarves, or let trail behind us like a bride's train.

So let me tell you the story of why we are in need of tails.

Once upon a time there were two beings, Huk and Tuk. We don't remember if they were both female, both male, or male and female. But that's immaterial. Huk and Tuk were friends — best friends — and loved doing many things together. They loved to walk in the woods. They loved to drink tea by a tiny pond in the middle of nowhere. And they loved to hold tails.

HUK and TUK

Fairy Tails

See, tails could communicate with intense subtlety and accuracy.

Now, without them, we need so many, so very many, many words, and still we cannot communicate the way we used to.

One day, Huk was trying to communicate some really subtle thing to Tuk, but Tuk couldn't understand.

Later, they walked in silence through the woods, not even knowing what the other was thinking or feeling.

They felt so disconnected from each other.

Then Tuk started to tell a tail — I mean tale — about dragons and lizards in faraway lands, all of whom still had tails.

Huk understood and started to feel connected again.

So Huk and Tuk came up with a plan.

They walked through the woods, they drank their leaf-tea, and...

they started telling tales.

These tales became what we now call fairy tales, although Huk and Tuk called them fairy tails, of course!

Tail-Theory

A very famous scientist came up with this amazing theory called string theory.

But for Huk and Tuk it is not all that amazing. After all, it was just a variation on tail-theory, really.

String theory says that everything is connected through strings. And if you think about it, tails are a kind of string.

In string theory — I mean tail-theory — everything is connected.

When everything is connected, everything has to do with everything else and every something is a part of something else. This keeps the world in balance, really. And this makes the world go around.

So how does this work then?

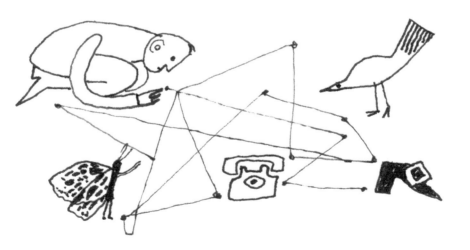

Knowing and Understanding

symphony

To hear a symphony instead of a cacophony, we need to connect the sounds we hear.

We have to develop a deeper understanding.

So Huk and Tuk thought about how it is that we know a lot, but do not understand a lot.

See, we can know a tree and know what it's good for, what its wood is good for and how we can use it for our benefit.

But to understand a tree is different. A tree is a million things, since it is connected to everything in the world around it — the air, the soil, the creatures

understanding a tree

So now we have to develop the understanding of how to become wise on our own and in our relationships with others and the world.

Trail Theory

Some of the many ways Huk and Tuk communicate now is through telling stories, through polyphonic or polylogic listening, and through understanding, not just smart-mindedness.

And there is another way to connect, too, through realizing you are a part of this miraculous universe.

heliocentric
world

Although we know we are a part of this miraculous universe, we rarely act on our knowledge of this fact, because we lack the understanding of what this means.

See, there are trails, which are essentially paths created by tails a long, long time ago.

Creatures dragged their tails through the woods behind them and over the centuries, trails formed.

These trails are not just to make it easy for you to walk through the woods, for they also allow you to absorb the awe and wonder of the world around you and the universe even, when you look up at the shooting stars — the meteors and the trails they leave behind.

Postscript

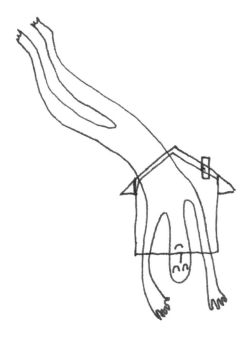

In these stories, Huk and Tuk have tried to point to ways we might be able to reconnect to this beautiful world we live in and to each other.

Now we have completely different tails, visible and invisible, wires and WiFis and such.

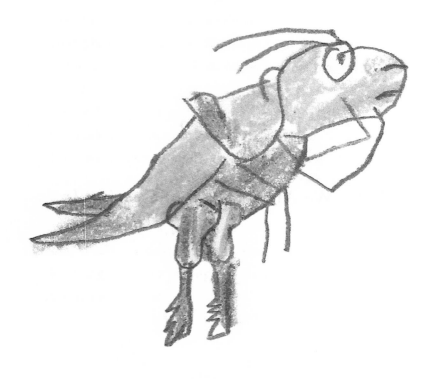

by Diego Gonzales

Why We Are in Need of Sharing In

— *It's Mine* by Leo Lionni —

Huk and Tuk decided to go to the middle of nowhere to have their cup of tea and tell each other tales.

They loved going to the middle of nowhere, because there is so much room there for our imagination.

Telling tales made them feel connected, sort of like how they felt connected when they had actual tails.

It was a bright sunny day, and Huk and Tuk decided to sit down by a pond called Rainbow Pond, which was named after the pond in a famous tale by Leo Lionni — the greatest of tale-tellers.

You know, said Huk, there's an interesting story about this pond. Do you know it?

No, said Tuk.

Well, Huk began, a long time ago, three quarrelsome frogs — Milton, Rupert and Lydia — lived on an island in this pond.

They fought all day long.

About what? asked Tuk.

You wouldn't believe it, said Huk, but Lydia thought the air was hers and hers alone. And Rupert thought the earth belonged to him and him alone. And Milton thought the water belonged solely to him.

But why? asked Tuk, looking confused.

They kept arguing, continued Huk, saying the earth is mine, the air is mine, the water is mine!

All this quarreling started to annoy a friendly toad named Toad who lived on the other side of the island. One day, totally fed up, he hopped over and told these three frogs to stop bickering. But they didn't listen to him.

Then there was a heavy rainstorm and it started to flood their little island in the middle of Rainbow Pond. The island got smaller and smaller, and the frogs got scared. They had nowhere to go. But then they spotted a rock and gathered on it. Huddled together, they trembled from cold and fright.

They felt better being close together as they clung to each other for dear life.

When the rain stopped and the water receded, they noticed to their utter amazement that the rock was not a rock. It was Toad who had saved them.

That's a really nice tale, said Tuk. It's a good story to make you feel connected to each other.

But there's more, said Huk. Listen! Those quarrelsome frogs now started sharing the water, the earth and the air. They jumped into the water together, they leaped after butterflies together and they finally rested in the weeds together. They were happy frogs now. And Toad was happy too, because the island was finally quiet and peaceful.

I never knew there was such an interesting story about Rainbow Pond, said Tuk. First they shared their fears, and then they shared what they originally thought was theirs alone.

That's right, said Huk. I guess they figured out sharing was more fun.

Soon Huk and Tuk fell asleep on the side of Rainbow Pond. The sun had made them sleepy.

After waking up, Tuk started to think about the story and couldn't figure out why someone, in this case a frog named Lydia, would claim the air was hers. The air was not only hers. Don't we all need air? Don't we all need water and earth? And even though you might claim the air is yours, you're also going to need water and earth. That's probably why they quarreled all the time — because they also needed what the others had and claimed was only theirs too.

The question, thought Tuk, is how do I decide that something is mine? Do I decide that? Are there rules for what is mine and not mine? Can someone take what is mine and then claim it belongs to them?

I can decide my body and my thoughts and feelings are mine. But when I share my thoughts and feelings, they are no longer mine alone.

It seems that these frogs thought if they shared the air, the water and the earth, it wouldn't be theirs anymore. Is that what they were really afraid of? So many questions were swimming in Tuk's head.

When Huk woke up, Tuk looked at Huk and decided that sharing tails (or tales) really does make you feel more connected and closer to each other. And it makes you feel more you!

But, Tuk thought, we also trust each other.

Maybe the frogs didn't trust each other at first. Once they learned they could trust each other when they huddled together in the storm, they too were able to share things — and to share in things.

When they started to share in the world of air, earth and water, a world so much greater than they were, they weren't afraid of sharing, afraid of losing what they claimed was theirs.

But what if you share your thoughts and feelings with others and some people make fun of you or think your thoughts and feelings don't matter? Isn't it better not to share and just keep to yourself?

Maybe you can't share and "hold tails" with everyone. Huk and Tuk figured that out a long time ago. But maybe you can learn to "hold tails" with someone you didn't think you could, just like Lydia, Milton and Rupert did.

Tuk liked this tale about Rainbow Pond and liked sharing tales — and tails — with Huk.

Then one day, the tadpole grew two tiny legs. Hey, he said, I'm a frog.

Nonsense, the minnow said, last night you were a little fish just like me.

You can imagine how they argued and argued, until the tadpole finally concluded, frogs are frogs and fish is fish.

That didn't really settle the argument, did it? asked Huk.

No, not really, said Tuk.

Anyway, one day, this tadpole — a real frog now — decided to climb out of the pond and onto the bank.

The minnow, by the way, was all grown up too and was a full-fledged fish by now.

But the frog did not return, and the fish wondered where his friend had gone.

Then, with a splash, the frog returned to the pond one day and the fish was overjoyed to see his friend again.

The frog began to talk about everything he had seen — birds and cows and people.

The minnow — now a fish, remember — listened intently, but couldn't quite picture all these creatures the frog was talking about in his mind.

So, the birds have fins? the fish asked.

Oh, no! said the frog.

Do the cows have gills?

No, no! said the frog.

How about the people, do they have scales?

Nooo! cried the frog.

The fish was exhausted from trying to understand what his friend was talking about.

And the frog was exhausted from trying to explain what his friend couldn't seem to understand.

That's pretty sad, said Huk. I guess that explains frogs are frogs and fish is fish.

Yes, said Tuk, but listen...

The fish was so curious that he decided to see for himself what frog was talking about. So, one day, with a whack of his tail, he threw himself onto the bank.

In a matter of seconds, he couldn't breathe and could only cry out a feeble, help!

then maybe you get a better idea of how different different can be.

Oh, said Huk, this is exciting, imagine all these worlds out there we know nothing about and how much we can learn if we stop comparing things to what we know.

You know, said Huk, if you think about it, even plants make decisions, such as where to get the most nutrients out of the soil.

So anyway, Huk continued, Alexander and Willy were friends — best friends — when Alexander was a real mouse and Willy was not a real mouse.

Now, however, they could be best friends forever!

You know, said Tuk, I love this story because it's a great tale about the importance of friendship. I mean *real* friendship.

Real friendship is based on wanting the best for the other. Willy knew Alexander was sad, and he wanted to make him happy. That's why he told him about the lizard, so Alexander could become a wind-up mouse like him and be loved by everybody.

And then Alexander wanted the best for Willy. By changing him into a real mouse, he wouldn't be thrown out with the other toys. He wanted to save Willy and he wanted to save their friendship.

A real friendship is more than the sum of two friends.

And a not-real friendship? asked Huk

A not-real friendship is less than the sum of two friends.

And it's not always easy to tell the difference.

What do you mean? asked Huk.

Willy was Annie's favorite toy and everybody loved him. Yet, one day he was put in the box of toys ready to be thrown away, said Tuk.

Would they have thrown him out if the friendship was really real?

Yeah, that's a good question, said Huk. And you know, Tuk, come to think of it, up to this day I still have my favorite toy, a magic lizard and a purple pebble too!

Huk and Tuk arrived at Pebble Path when it started to get dark.

We should be heading back home, said Tuk. I'll make dinner.

He saw the bright sunshine, he noticed the earth sparkling with dew and he felt the crisp, fresh air as he went on down the road.

Huk and Tuk agreed with Grasshopper. The whole day is beautiful — morning, noon and night.

What Does It Mean to Be Included?

— *The Voyage* by Arnold Lobel —

Grasshopper didn't mind that he no longer belonged to the morning only club, but he didn't like the way the beetles had treated him.

He didn't like the way they excluded him from the club, calling him *stupid* and *dummy* and snatching his wreath and sign away like that.

Oh, said Huk, that reminds me of another story about Grasshopper.

The evening is young, said Tuk, so tell me this one too, before we turn in for the night.

This time, Huk said, Grasshopper came across a mosquito called Mosquito.

Oh, I think I know who you mean, said Tuk, Mosquito who takes riders in his little boat from one side of the puddle to the other?

Yes, but to Mosquito that puddle is a lake, said Huk.

Then we should call it Puddle Lake, suggested Tuk.

Mosquito had been carrying riders across Puddle Lake, Huk began, for as long as he could remember.

To get his riders across Puddle Lake safely, he had strict rules.

When Grasshopper got to Puddle Lake, which really just looked like a small puddle in the road to him, he met Mosquito.

Rules are rules, Mosquito told Grasshopper. You have to get into my boat if you want to safely get to the other side.

Grasshopper was a bit confused. He didn't want to offend Mosquito, but he knew he was way, way too big to get into the boat. Didn't Mosquito realize that?

He didn't, because he kept telling Grasshopper that rules are rules.

Grasshopper had looked and decided he could easily jump to the other side, but the beetles had been rude to Grasshopper and he wasn't going to be rude to Mosquito.

And besides, Grasshopper is not a rude kind of grasshopper.

So, what happened? asked Tuk.

Tuk was really curious how Grasshopper was going to solve this problem, because there was no way he could ever get into Mosquito's tiny boat, even if rules are rules.

Well, he could have just walked — or rather hopped — away, said Huk.

He could have ignored Mosquito and his rules altogether.

But he didn't do that.

Then, what *did* he do? asked Tuk.

What would you have done? asked Huk.

Tuk shook his head, not really knowing what to say.

Well, Grasshopper came up with a very wise idea, Huk told Tuk.

He picked up Mosquito's ferry and walked across Puddle Lake with it.

When Mosquito felt the boat moving, he called out, All aboard!

Mosquito got excited and told Grasshopper all about taking riders across for many years and how he was never afraid of storms and waves.

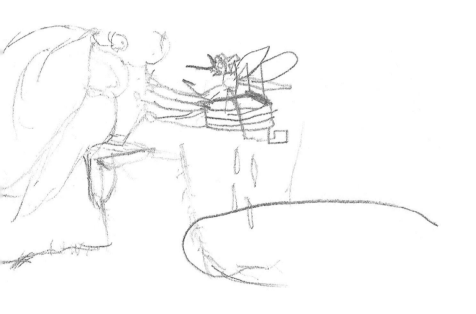

by Marc Guaro

Grasshopper listened to Mosquito.

When they got to the other side, Grasshopper put Mosquito's boat down.

Mosquito was proud to have safely carried Grasshopper across Puddle Lake and told him he now had to get back to get new riders.

Grasshopper thanked Mosquito for safely taking him across the lake.

Huh? said Tuk. How did Mosquito not realize that it was Grasshopper who had carried the boat across the lake?

His world only includes very small insects that can fit in his boat, said Huk, and his rules are to carry those creatures safely across Puddle Lake.

He can't see that his rules don't apply to Grasshopper. In his mind, Grasshopper should also get into the boat — if he wants to get to the other side, that is.

But rules don't always apply, said Tuk.

No, of course not, said Huk. They only apply in certain cases — cases the rules are made for.

But Mosquito thought they applied to *everything* and *everyone*, said Tuk. It reminds me of the fish who thought the way of the watery world applied to everybody too, and so birds and cows and people must all have fins, and scales and gills too.

Yeah, folks get carried away, said Huk, and forget what rules are for. They just remember, rules are rules, like Mosquito did.

Grasshopper decided to respect Mosquito and Mosquito's rules, even when they didn't apply to him. So he picked up the boat instead of hopping across Puddle Lake.

And Grasshopper even thanked Mosquito for taking him safely across the lake.

He thanked Mosquito? asked Tuk.

Yes, said Huk, perhaps simply to be kind to Mosquito and to include him in the journey across Puddle Lake.

Hmm, said Huk, I like that idea of being kind and including him, just because.

by Amaris Rodriguez

Why We Are in Need of Making Choices with Our Eyes Wide Open

— *Cookies* by Arnold Lobel —

The next morning, Huk and Tuk set out for the hills nearby.

I have a question, said Tuk. How do we figure out when rules apply and when they don't? I mean, obviously Mosquito's rules didn't apply to Grasshopper because he was way too big for Mosquito's ferry.

But I'm sure there are times it is not so obvious.

Like when? asked Huk.

Let's say there is a rule to not eat animals, said Tuk. But what if you are in a situation where the only way to *survive* is to eat an animal?

Do the rules apply only to everyday life, or to situations of life and death, too?

Well, said Huk, I'd rather die than eat an animal.

And I, said Tuk, would most certainly kill and eat an animal in order to survive.

How does one decide...? Huk wondered.

How does one decide if a rule applies to you or not? And would Tuk get in trouble for not following the rule because Tuk desperately wanted to stay alive?

Is there a rule about rules? Huk asked.

Good question, said Tuk. Are we responsible for deciding whether to follow a rule or not? And does it mean we are not personally responsible if we blindly follow the rule? I mean, if I follow the rule, is the rule ultimately responsible for how I act?

Oh my, said Huk, this is complicated. I guess, if it's my decision to follow the rule, it is ultimately my responsibility, too. I mean, I can't hide behind the rule and blame the rule if things don't work out right. I can only blame myself for following a rule I should not have followed.

So is the rule about rules, that whatever the rule, I am ultimately responsible for following it or not? asked Huk.

That sounds about right, concluded Tuk.

Hey, said Tuk, do you remember our buddies Frog and Toad, who live near Pebble Path close to where the magic lizard lives?

Yes, of course I remember Frog and Toad, said Huk. What about them?

Well, Tuk continued, there's a funny story going around about how Frog and Toad were trying to figure out what rules to use to stop eating Toad's delicious fresh-baked cookies so they wouldn't get sick.

Tell me, said Huk.

One day, said Tuk, Toad decided to bake some cookies and bring them over to Frog's house so they could enjoy them together.

Toad had made a lot of cookies. They were so good that they couldn't stop eating them.

At some point, Frog pointed out that if they didn't stop, they'd start feeling sick.

While they both agreed they should really stop, they couldn't help eating one more last cookie and then one more very last cookie after that.

So, this rule was obviously not working. Something else was needed.

Toad had agreed with Frog that they needed to stop eating the cookies, but how do you stop doing something you really want to do?

by Adriana Perez

Frog explained that you need willpower. Because willpower is the rule that makes you stop doing what you don't want to stop doing.

Toad had been quiet for a bit and then said, Like not eating any more very last cookies?

That's right, Frog said, put the cookies in a box and then I'll put them high up on the shelf. That'll work. Then we can follow our rule.

But we can break the rule by taking the box down and opening the box, Toad suggested.

Well, said Frog, then we'll tie a string around the box. Then we can follow the rule.

What good is a rule if you can take the box down from the shelf, cut the string and open the box? You can see where this was going, said Tuk. Nowhere!

So, I guess, said Huk, they couldn't follow their own rules?

Does that mean they didn't have any willpower?

I'm not so sure, said Tuk, because they seemed to be trying. They were thinking of ways to make themselves stick to the rule of eating no more cookies.

by Johnny Tejeda Rodriguez

But then Frog had a bright idea, Tuk continued. He took the box outside and emptied it, calling out, Hey birds, here are cookies!

And guess what? Gone were the cookies. Just like that.

Okay, said Huk, there are no more cookies to eat. Does that mean they followed their own rule? I'm not so sure.

Throwing the cookies to the birds took the problem away and so the need for willpower didn't come into play anymore either.

But didn't it take willpower to throw the cookies out? asked Tuk.

I think it's more like following a rule with your eyes closed, said Huk, because they didn't have to make any effort to not eat the cookies anymore. With the cookies gone, the rule to not eat any more cookies was also gone. And the willpower was gone too. Gone!

So, is it self-deception to follow rules with your eyes closed? asked Tuk.

I am going to backc ackaee

by Alexa Garcia

Self-deception? asked Huk. Explain.

You think you're following the rules and you make-believe you're following the rules, said Tuk, but you're not following anything, because there's nothing to follow.

Tuk was sounding very philosophical.

How come there's nothing to follow? asked Huk.

Because, said Tuk, if you get rid of the problem, there is nothing to follow.

It's like that ancient tale about Oedipus. Remember? The oracle of Delphi told Oedipus that he was going to kill his father and marry his mother.

So to get rid of the problem — kind of like what Frog did by throwing the cookies to the birds — he left his home in the city of Corinth and fled to a faraway place called Thebes. That way he could not kill his father and marry his mother, who both lived in Corinth.

But Thebes is exactly where he ended up killing his *real* father and marrying his *real* mother, who both lived in Thebes.

Having been warned by an oracle that their son would slay his father, Oedipus's mother had abandoned Oedipus when he was born. A shepherd had found him and brought him to Corinth, where the king and queen of Corinth adopted him.

So that's how Oedipus left Corinth and ended up in Thebes.

Getting rid of a problem is not solving it, Huk and Tuk agreed.

So, said Huk, Frog and Toad should have found a way to keep the cookies *and* not eat them.

Does that mean that willpower only makes sense when your eyes are wide open? asked Tuk.

Yes, said Huk, your eyes wide open and the bowl of cookies right in front of them.

If you blindly follow the rules, you don't have to be or feel responsible for anything.

You make yourself *believe* you are being responsible, because you are doing your duty by following the rules, but in fact you are not taking any responsibility at all. You're just blindly following the rules. That's a cop-out really, and that's called self-deception.

Oh, thought Tuk, who was getting to understand how self-deception works.

So Huk and Tuk decided that if you don't want to deceive yourself, you should keep your eyes wide open.

They knew that when you walk through the woods or up on the hills, you have to keep your eyes wide open. And it really seems to be a good rule overall. There are always twists and turns in life no matter where you go.

Sometimes it seems so much easier to just go along with some rule and not think too much about it, Huk decided. And when someone questions you, you just say, well, I followed the rule the way I was supposed to.

Figuring things out for yourself is a whole different can of worms — I mean bowl of cookies, Huk added with a smile.

Huk and Tuk liked this tale and — taking full responsibility now — figured they should go home and bake some delicious cookies.

by Laisha Delgado

Chapter 3

Why We Are in Need of Dreams

Introduction

Huk and Tuk discover why we now need tales, and they show us how tales can take the place of tails by helping us reconnect to the mystery of life. They love sharing tales with each other and discussing what they think and feel about them. Through this sharing, they find out in this chapter why we are in need of dreams. See, dreams — in a mysterious way — also help us to reconnect to the world around us.

Dreams are kind of funny because they seem to come out of nowhere.

But where is nowhere, you ask? I don't know, really, but I think our imaginations know somehow, because they can create things out of nowhere.

By the way, that's how Huk and Tuk came into existence. They materialized out of nowhere too.

See, dreams can spark our curiosity (by imagining the other side of things) and ignite our fantasies (by imagining a world that can lift our spirits) and light up our creativity (by imagining the beauty expressed in art and music).

Or perhaps it's the other way around. Maybe curiosity, fantasy and creativity spark dreams. What do you think? Either way, this is what these stories are about.

And did you know that one of the real geniuses of this world, Albert Einstein, believed that imagination is more important than knowledge? Think about it: Without imagination, we cannot create anything new. How dull would it be if everything were the same all the time?

Oh, and there's something else I need to tell you: Huk and Tuk also learn how important it is to keep your eyes wide open. Have you ever taken a walk through the woods? When you walk through the woods, you need to be able to see where you're going. You have to figure out what paths to take. Life is sort of like that too. In order to figure out what paths to take in life, or even what paths you could take in life, you need your eyes to be wide open. Curiosity and imagination, as these next tales will show you, help you do that.

These tales are about the role dreams play in our lives. Dreams are like a third eye that helps us see things in so many *new* ways. That's really fascinating.

When we lost our tails, the mystery of life was sort of lost too. Thankfully, tales and dreams can help reconnect us with that mystery.

Why We Are in Need of Curiosity

— *Tillie and the Wall* by Leo Lionni —

Huk was over at Tuk's place enjoying the cool summer breeze while sitting on the little patio that Tuk had built.

Life can be so perfect at times for no particular reason.

Tuk lived on a hill, and from Tuk's house you could see the remnants of an old wall. Nobody knew why the wall was there, but everyone assumed it had served some purpose a long time ago.

Do you know what that wall was for? Huk asked.

No, Tuk replied. I've never really paid attention to it. I guess it's just always been there.

You know, Tuk continued, that reminds me of a tale about that exact thing: a wall that no one really paid attention to. There was this little mouse named Tillie who was the youngest in her family of mice. What was special about Tillie was that she would see things nobody else ever did.

How did she do that? Huk asked.

She had her eyes wide open! Tuk exclaimed.

So, what did Tillie see that nobody else saw? Huk wanted to know. Really small things?

No, Tuk said, that's the surprising thing. Tillie noticed this humongous wall that everybody else just ignored. It was like they didn't even *see* that it was there.

I guess they figured it was part of the landscape, said Huk, and so they didn't give it a second thought. Just like you with that wall at the bottom of the hill.

Yes, exactly, said Tuk, but that's how Tillie was different. She always gave things a second thought. She was curious by nature.

And so, she was also really curious about the wall. She would always stare at the wall and wonder what was on the other side.

At night, when everybody else was asleep, Tillie would lie awake and imagine what could be on the other side of the wall — maybe there's a beautiful world over there with fantastical animals and plants. Who knows!

Tillie got so curious, Tuk continued, that she decided she *must* find out for herself what was on the other side of this huge wall.

by Yesenia Perez

She asked some of her friends to help her climb over the wall. She instructed them to stand on each other's shoulders, but even when they all stood as tall as they could and she climbed up to stand on her topmost friend's shoulders, Tillie still couldn't reach the top of the wall. The wall was *too tall*.

But Tillie was determined. This time, she decided to use a long rusty nail to poke a hole in the wall so she could peep through it and so her friends could peep through it too. They worked so hard trying to make a hole in the wall with the nail, but it didn't work. The wall was *too thick*.

Then she thought that they could go around the wall. Tillie and her friends walked and walked, looking for the end of the wall, but the wall was *too long*.

Her friends gave up, but Tillie didn't. Tillie got more and more curious and determined.

I guess I would too, Huk interjected.

Now this is where the story gets interesting, Tuk said, because one day Tillie noticed a worm digging a hole not far from the wall.

A light bulb went off in her little mouse head, and she thought, Why hadn't anyone thought of this before?

Because Tillie's eyes were open with curiosity, she could see that the worm was showing her another way to the other side of the wall. And this time, Tillie thought, it may actually work.

She was so excited — wouldn't you be, Huk? — that she immediately started digging. Mice are really good at digging, so off she went.

She dug a long, deep tunnel under the wall. It was pitch black and very scary. She had no idea where she was going.

I think she's super brave, said Huk. Would you just go dig into the middle of nowhere? I know I wouldn't!

Maybe curiosity makes you brave, Tuk considered. This little mouse was on a mission and nothing was going to stop her.

Well, she finally made it to the other side, and you would not believe what she saw.

What did she see? asked Huk, who was totally wrapped up in the story and a bit scared too.

She saw mice, said Tuk. She saw a mouse family just like her own mouse family. Imagine that: after going on a long dig, you find creatures on the other side of the wall who are just like you.

The on-the-other-side-of-the-wall mice were also surprised and excited. They welcomed Tillie with a grand celebration.

And you know what else? Tuk said. Now these on-the-other-side-of-the-wall mice wanted to see what was on the other side of their wall too, and one by one, they followed Tillie back through the tunnel to her side of the wall.

That's a really interesting story, Huk decided. Tillie's imagination made her curious about what was on the other side of the wall — curious enough to try to find ways to get to the other side of it. And since she always gave things a second thought, she never gave up.

That's true, Tuk agreed. Her friends showed some interest, but they gave up after the first few things they tried didn't work. Only Tillie kept on trying to figure out what she could do to get to the other side.

Exactly! Huk said. And that's why she noticed the worm and discovered that tunneling was another method she could try.

And she took a real risk, Huk continued. Her own family of mice and the on-the-other-side-of-the-wall family of mice really admired her for what she did. And just look at the new world that opened up for all of them!

Tuk decided that both families now had a family on either side of the wall. Who would have guessed!

Why We Are in Need of Imagination

— *Cornelius* by Leo Lionni —

Huk and Tuk were getting a bit cold sitting outside on Tuk's patio, so they moved indoors and made a nice cup of hot tea.

Huk looked at Tuk and asked, do you remember Cornelius?

Hmm, Tuk responded, Cornelius who?

Cornelius, the young crocodile who walked upright, Huk said.

Upright, you say? Tuk asked. No, I don't think so.

Cornelius was a young croc who had just crawled out of his egg and onto the sandy beach along the river, Huk continued.

But unlike his siblings, who walked on all fours, Cornelius walked upright on his two hind legs.

That's peculiar, Tuk said.

That's right, said Huk, who went on to explain how as Cornelius grew taller and stronger — still walking on his two hind legs — he could see things no one else could. He was able to see way beyond the bushes.

And with his eyes wide open, Huk continued, he could see so far away. But his family was not interested in what he could see and just said things like, So what's so good about that? And when Cornelius could see the fish in the river from his higher vantage point, all his family said was, So what?

No one showed any interest in all the things Cornelius could see, or even any curiosity. He was so hurt and disappointed because his family didn't seem to care what he could do. And so he wandered off.

Well, Tillie's family and friends never made fun of her, Tuk thought. Her friends even tried to help her get to the other side. They certainly weren't the sticks-in-the-mud these crocs were. Blah!

So where did he go? Tuk wanted to know.

I'm not too sure, Huk said. I don't think the tale says, but it does say that soon after he wandered off, he saw a monkey sitting under a tree.

Cornelius, still excited about the world of wonders he could see while walking upright, said to

by Ricardo Alvarado

the monkey, I can walk upright, you know, and see far away.

The monkey responded by saying, And I can stand on my head. And I can hang from my tail.

Cornelius was impressed. Cornelius could walk upright, but he could not do those things. So he asked the monkey to teach him.

The monkey was eager to help Cornelius learn his tricks. Because Cornelius could imagine himself doing those things, Huk said, he decided to practice and practice with the monkey's help. It took some work from both Cornelius and the monkey, though. Crocs are not meant to do these kinds of things. And maybe that's why the crocodile family showed no interest whatsoever. Crocs do what crocs do, and that's that.

Did Cornelius learn how to do what the monkey could do? Tuk asked.

Cornelius was determined, Huk said, and finally he learned how to stand on his head and hang from his tail, just as the monkey had taught him.

Cornelius was super proud now that he could do these tricks too, Huk continued. And so, he walked back to the beach along the river to show his family what he'd learned.

Uh-oh, said Tuk, that doesn't sound good.

Why? Huk asked.

Before he wandered off, Tuk said, his family couldn't care less that he could do things they could not, so why would they care now?

Maybe his family doesn't show any interest because they might see him as a show-off, Tuk continued, and maybe they even worry that he thinks he is better than they are.

Do you think he's a show-off? Tuk asked.

Huk took a sip of tea and responded, I don't know what his family thinks, but *I* don't think Cornelius is a show-off. Cornelius was simply excited about what he could do, and he really wanted to learn these tricks from the monkey.

He could imagine himself learning new things all the time. I mean, when the monkey said to him that he could stand on his head and hang from his tail, Cornelius *could* have responded like his family did by saying something like, so what? Or, what's so good about that? Or, I'm a croc and you're a monkey and we cannot do the same things.

But because he could imagine himself being able to do these monkey tricks too, he asked the monkey to teach him and help him accomplish these things crocodiles simply don't do. Have *you* ever seen a crocodile hang from its tail?

I get it, said Tuk, because when Cornelius told his family he could see things far away when he walked upright, they too could have asked him how to walk upright, so they could see far away too.

I think Cornelius just wanted to share what he knew, Huk said, and that's also why he was eager to go back to the beach along the river where his family lived.

So, what happened then? How did his family react? Tuk wanted to know.

Well, they reacted exactly the way you would expect such a stick-in-the-mud family to react: When Cornelius showed them that he could stand on his head and hang from his tail, all they could say was — once again — so what?

As you would expect, Huk said, Cornelius was — once again — hurt and disappointed. He decided to leave these uninspired crocs to themselves and to go back to be with the monkey. At least he and the monkey were friends, and they could share their cool tricks.

But as he started to walk away — still upright — he glanced over his shoulder and saw something amazing: His brothers and sisters were falling over each other trying to stand on their heads and hang from their tails.

Really! Tuk exclaimed. They were jealous of Cornelius? Did they really just want to be able to do all the things Cornelius could do too?

Huk nodded and said, it seems so.

Then why didn't they ask Cornelius to teach them just like Cornelius had asked the monkey to teach him?

That's an interesting question, Huk said. What do you think?

Maybe his sisters and brothers did kind of admire Cornelius but did not want to look like fools trying to do the things Cornelius did, Tuk replied. Sometimes we don't want to try new things because we don't want to feel embarrassed when we can't do them.

But somehow Cornelius doesn't really care if he looks like a fool. He just keeps on trying and keeps on practicing until he can do these tricks too.

Huk smiled. That sounds a little like when Tillie found a way to get to the other side of the wall.

How so? Tuk asked.

Well, Tuk, just like Tillie, Cornelius never gave up, Huk said.

And they didn't give up because they were curious and could imagine things beyond what they knew already. And a whole new world opened up because of it.

by Yesenia Perez

Why We Are in Need of Nighttime Dreams

— *The Dream* by Arnold Lobel —

The next day, Huk and Tuk went to see a play called "The Dream."

Huk and Tuk know that everyone has dreams big and small, and dreams influence how we think and feel and sometimes even how we live our lives. So they decided that seeing a play about dreams would be very inspiring.

When Huk and Tuk got to the theater, Frog and Toad were there. Toad was going to be on stage that night. Frog was in the audience and was eagerly awaiting his best friend's performance.

Soon Toad appeared on stage. He looked like he belonged in a Shakespearean play with his incredibly colorful outfit, boots and wide-rimmed hat with a plume hanging from his chapeau. He was a toad of consequence, and everyone in the audience was in awe.

Huk looked at Tuk and nodded in admiration. This is going to be some play, Huk whispered.

Then they heard a loud voice announce: Presenting the greatest toad in the world.

Frog, seated in a front-row seat, started clapping. He agreed that Toad was indeed the greatest toad ever.

Toad took a deep bow and sat at the piano.

The voice then announced: Toad will now play the piano very well.

Frog, who could not help himself, cried out, Hooray for Toad!

Toad started playing the piano and was magnificent. He didn't miss a note.

Frog, cried Toad, can you play the piano like this?

No, said Frog.

When Toad looked into the audience, he spotted his friend Frog.

Huk and Tuk noticed that Toad looked puzzled after he saw Frog, so they looked over. Tuk leaned over to Huk and whispered, does Frog look smaller to you?

by Adrian Cacho

I'm not sure, Huk replied, looking a bit concerned. Then Huk whispered, I thought this play was going to be about dreams.

Maybe we should wait and see, Tuk whispered.

Again, the same voice came on and announced: Toad will now walk on a high wire and he will not fall down.

Huk and Tuk saw Toad perform this dangerous feat with ease.

Toad called out to Frog and asked if this was something he could do. Again, Frog said no, he couldn't.

Huk and Tuk noticed that after Toad was done walking on the high wire, he looked into the audience at Frog. Toad looked worried. Huk and Tuk followed Toad's gaze to where Frog was sitting. Frog seemed smaller still. Then they too looked really worried. Huk and Tuk didn't know what was going on.

Was this all a dream?

Huk and Tuk had gone to see a play called "The Dream," or so they thought. Were they now the ones dreaming?

by Ethan Hernandez

How about the rest of the audience? Were they watching a play, or were they *in* a play?

The announcer came on again and said: Toad will now dance, and it will be wonderful.

When Huk and Tuk looked over to where Frog sat, there was no one there. Frog had disappeared.

Huk gasped. What just happened, Tuk? Frog is gone!

This was certainly the strangest play they had ever seen, and they got scared.

But it wasn't just Huk and Tuk who got scared.

Frog! Toad cried. Frog, where are you? Toad sounded desperate.

Let's go home, Huk suggested. I don't like this play. This play is a nightmare, not a dream.

Meanwhile, Toad panicked, and while the announcer started to say something like, And now the greatest toad will..., Toad ran off the stage looking for Frog.

At that point, Huk and Tuk got up and left the theater. They were not interested in the ending.

When they got outside, Huk looked at Tuk and said, Oh boy, that was weird, and Huk gave Tuk a big hug to make sure Tuk was real and hadn't disappeared.

I can't wait to get home and have some hot chocolate to calm my nerves, Huk said.

When they were settled in at Huk's place, drinking their hot chocolate, Huk asked, But why did Frog get smaller and smaller?

I think, Tuk replied, that maybe when someone boasts about how they are the best, it makes their friends feel small.

And when Toad realized that he might have lost his friend in the process of bragging about how great he was, he panicked. He didn't want to lose his best friend Frog.

So "The Dream" was really about how important friendships are — maybe even how they are the most important? asked Huk.

As they drank their hot chocolate in silence, Huk and Tuk both looked discombobulated. They were imagining how Toad felt not seeing Frog in the audience anymore. What if they each looked over at the other and there was no one there?

Tuk thought, What if Huk disappeared?

Huk thought, What if Tuk disappeared?

They had to stop imagining what this might feel like. This was horrible!

It wasn't until they had finished their hot chocolate that they looked at each other, so happy they were sitting there together as best friends who wouldn't *dream* of being without each other.

Huk and Tuk are still not quite sure whether they had been watching a play called "The Dream" or actually dreaming they were watching a play called "The Dream." Whatever it was, it had made them aware and woke them up — with eyes wide open — to how very important real friendship is.

Why We Are in Need of Daytime Dreams

— *Frederick* by Leo Lionni —

One morning, Tuk went over to Huk's place for breakfast. They had some nice warm toast with jam and hot coffee.

It was frigid out. The cold made Tuk think of a tale about a mouse named Frederick. Huk, Tuk said, do you know the tale about Frederick the daydreamer mouse? Frederick who didn't prepare for winter in the same way the other mice did?

No, said Huk, I don't know about any daydreamer mouse. Tell me about him.

Frederick, Tuk began, lived with his mouse family in the crumbling wall below my house. I've seen them scurrying about many times. The story starts in the fall when all the mice were gathering supplies like nuts and wheat and straw and preparing for the winter months. All the mice except Frederick, that is. Frederick didn't join them.

Didn't he help out? Huk asked. Did he just loaf around instead?

That's exactly what he was accused of doing, Tuk replied. He sat in the sun instead.

Why? Huk interjected.

Frederick told the others that he was gathering sunrays for the cold dark days of winter. He reassured them that he too was hard at work. But they didn't seem to believe him.

Would you believe Frederick, Huk? Or would you accuse him of being lazy and of making up silly excuses to not help out?

Not knowing quite what to say, Huk did not reply. It seemed to Huk that Frederick should have helped out, but then again, why not believe him when he said he was hard at work too?

While he sat on a stone, staring at the meadow, Tuk continued, Frederick told the other mice that he was gathering colors for when the days became gray and dreary.

So, was he working hard like the other mice or not? Huk asked.

Well, that depends on what you mean by work, I guess, Tuk replied.

That didn't sound all that convincing to Huk. Work meant *doing* things, like gathering nuts and storing them in the crevices of the wall. Sitting on a stone and gathering sunrays or colors didn't sound like work at all.

So, what else did Frederick do — or rather, not do? Huk wanted to know.

Tuk told Huk that Frederick once seemed half asleep, and the other mice thought he was dreaming. Are you dreaming? the mice asked. Oh no! Frederick said. I am gathering words for when nobody has anything left to say during the long, cold winter.

Finally, the winter set in and the mice disappeared into their cozy little hideout in the wall.

For a while, the straw kept them warm, and they had lots to eat. They told each other stories about foxes and such, and they were happy.

But as the winter carried on, they had less and less to eat. It seemed colder than before, and no one felt like telling stories anymore.

But then they remembered Frederick and asked him about *his* supplies.

Huk was curious how this was going to play out and urged Tuk to continue.

Frederick told the other mice to close their eyes and imagine the warm glow of the sunrays, said Tuk.

As Frederick spoke of the sun, the other mice did start feeling a little better when they imagined how the sun warmed their bodies. They weren't sure if it was Frederick's words as he spoke or some kind of magic that caused it.

Then Frederick told them to imagine the colors of the blue periwinkles, the red poppies, the yellow wheat and the green leaves. Suddenly, the winter didn't seem so gray anymore.

Huk was impressed. The power of imagination was nothing to sneeze at. It really could make you feel better.

The mice were impressed too and asked Frederick about the words he had gathered up. Then he recited a poem he had created in his head from the words he had gathered.

The mice were convinced that Frederick's hard work *had* paid off and *had* helped them all get through the rough, cold winter after all.

Huk liked this story and decided that without imagination, life would be quite unbearable, even if you had enough to eat.

So, is imagination something like food for thought? Huk wondered. Huk thought that expression said it all — imagination was a kind of food for the mind and, just like food, it helped them get through the bitter, cold winter.

As though Tuk could read Huk's thoughts, Tuk said, Imagination creates thoughts and feelings from what we can't always see; it exists in our mind. I mean, we need a mind's eye to see it. And with their mind's eye, the family of mice was able to somehow feel the glow of the warm sun, see the beautiful and vibrant colors of the flowers and feel the soothing effects of Frederick's poetry.

In that way, Frederick helped his family get through the winter, not by collecting food or straw, but by transporting them through their imaginations to a world way beyond the bitter cold.

by Nayeli Garcia

Why We Are in Need of Creativity

— *Matthew's Dream* by Leo Lionni —

After Huk and Tuk's strange experience at the theater, they decided to visit the Metropolitan Mouse Museum — the MeMo Museum for short.

They had heard about the great artwork of a new artist by the name of Matthew and were eager to go see his famous paintings.

Huk and Tuk made a delicious lunch to take along, and then they headed to the MeMo Museum.

On the way, Huk told Tuk a little bit about this new artist.

Matthew, Huk began, was an only child in his mouse family. And in a corner of the attic where they lived, he had gathered a bunch of stuff — books, magazines, pieces of an old lamp and a broken doll. They called it "Matthew's corner."

Matthew's family was very, very poor and could not afford nice things.

His parents would ask Matthew repeatedly, What do you want to be when you grow up? They were secretly hoping Matthew would say his life's dream was to become a doctor or lawyer and they would become very, very rich and be able to afford Parmesan cheese and other delicacies.

Matthew was curious about the world beyond the attic where his family lived, and he said, I don't know what I want to be. I want to see the world.

That didn't sound overly encouraging to Matthew's family, but Matthew was still young and in school, so they didn't push the issue.

One day, Huk continued, Matthew and his classmates went to the MeMo Museum.

The mouse artwork was spectacular. The portraits of famous mice, the still lifes of fruit and Parmesan cheese, and the landscapes of mountains and rivers enthralled Matthew. Then his class came to a gallery of abstract art. Matthew had never seen art like that before, and he found it intriguing and exciting.

As he looked at the abstract art, Matthew realized that the world he'd always wanted to see was right there

by Edgar Parada

in front of him. This world was alive with vibrant colors, and with all kinds of shapes dancing across the canvas.

While Matthew was strolling through the abstract art gallery, he met a mouse named Nicoletta, who also thought the art was wonderful and inspiring.

When Matthew got home from his field trip to the MeMo Museum, he felt so happy. The museum had felt like home. The paintings he'd seen had excited him and made sense to him.

That night, he dreamed that the world had become one huge painting, and he and Nicoletta walked through it hand in hand.

Let's stay here forever, he whispered to her in his dream.

When he woke up, he found himself back in his little corner of the attic. All the beauty in his dream had vanished. He felt alone and lonely, and he cried.

But then his little eyes suddenly opened wide, and everything started to change around him. Instead of junk, he saw colors and shapes similar to what he had seen in the museum. The doll's hair was golden and her dress a beautiful green. The magazine covers

by Adrian Cacho

were splashed with vibrant colors, and spreading out from the cobwebs were subtle silver threads. It was as though magic had turned his little corner into a whole new world. It had come *alive* too.

Then he ran to his parents, so the story goes, and told them he wanted to become a painter. And that's what he did! He worked hard and became the best painter he could be.

Wow! said Tuk. He made his dream come true.

That's right, Huk said. Matthew lived out his dream: He ended up seeing the world by becoming a famous painter. He also married Nicoletta. And, to his family's delight, he could afford Parmesan cheese, which they happily feasted on every night.

His most famous painting is in the museum we're going to today, said Huk. It's called "My Dream."

Hmm, said Tuk, so not only did Matthew become a creative artist, his creativity helped him to see the world beyond his little corner up in the attic. Creativity opened up his eyes wide and his little world became so big.

by Marcos Maldonado

But what *is* creativity, Huk? Tuk wanted to know.

Well, said Huk, creativity, I think, is like imagination and curiosity and dreaming because it creates something that wasn't there before.

I'm not sure I understand, said Tuk. How does it work?

If you think about it, Huk continued, Tillie was curious about what was behind that huge wall and discovered a whole new world existed beyond it. Cornelius imagined himself doing tricks nobody in his family had ever thought of doing. You see what I'm saying?

I think so, said Tuk. Frederick gathered up a world of colors and warm sunrays and words that helped his family get beyond the world of the bitter, cold winter. And Matthew created a whole new world beyond his little corner in the attic.

I see, Tuk concluded. They did all create something out of nothing.

Why We Are in Need of Art

— Geraldine, The Music Mouse by Leo Lionni —

It was a long day at the MeMo Museum. When Huk and Tuk finally got home, they cooked a wonderful meal. It had so many different colored vegetables in it that it too looked like a colorful abstract painting.

Art is so inspiring, Huk said. It makes everything come alive, don't you think?

It actually does, Tuk said. Let me tell you about another great artist by the name of Geraldine. She makes music come alive.

Geraldine is a musician. Have you heard of her?

I have, said Huk. I have heard her music. She plays the flute, and her music is like a dream.

Geraldine was a mouse who had never heard music before, so how she became a musician is an interesting story, Tuk said.

Huk was confused. Could she not hear the sound of music, or was there simply never any music in her life?

The tale doesn't say, Tuk answered. She could hear noises and the peeping of other mice, but music? Never!

Anyway, Tuk continued, Geraldine lived in a big house, and this house had a pantry.

Amazing, Huk interjected, because mice love pantries.

That's so true, returned Tuk. So one day when Geraldine went looking in the pantry, she saw a huge piece of Parmesan cheese. Her eyes grew big, and she desperately wanted to take the cheese to her hideout, but she didn't know how to do it.

She decided to tell her friends about the cheese. That's what friends are for.

Friends are for helping you steal cheese? Huk asked dubiously.

Or, Tuk said, friends are for helping you out.

Helping you out to do what? Huk persisted.

Anyway, Tuk continued, Geraldine's friends were eager to help, and off they all marched to the pantry. Parmesan could not be passed up.

by Edgar Parada

With a lot of community effort, they were able to push, pull and drag the huge piece of cheese to Geraldine's hideout.

Immediately, she went to the top of the block of cheese and started nibbling piece by piece, chunk after chunk.

Her friends, excited to see that much Parmesan cheese, started carrying off bits of the cheese. What a treat this was!

But when Geraldine looked at the cheese, she noticed that the shapes of two giant mouse ears had appeared where she had been nibbling away. She seemed to have sculpted the cheese into what looked like a mouse without even realizing it.

And as she kept on nibbling away, she saw that the mouse was holding its tail to its lips, the way someone would hold a flute. Remember, though, Geraldine had never seen or heard a flute.

So how did she do it? Huk asked.

It's a mystery, Tuk replied. She had created an incredible sculpture without even realizing, and somehow the mouse in the sculpture was playing an instrument she didn't know anything about.

by Ricardo Alvarado

Not surprisingly, Geraldine was exhausted from all the work and soon fell asleep.

And not long after that, she was awakened by some wonderful sounds — sounds that seemed to come from the mouse's tail flute. Was she dreaming?

Well, was she dreaming? Huk asked.

The story is that she was wide awake when she heard those beautiful sounds, Tuk replied. Or she at least felt wide awake in her dream. And she could clearly hear the music coming from the mouse sculpture.

She was in awe.

But then another strange thing happened, Tuk continued. As the night slowly turned to day, the music started to fade as well. But every night, when it started to get dark, the music started once again. This went on for several days.

And then Geraldine started to hear the music during the day too. It was lingering in her head, and she started to recognize the melodies.

Her friends, who had run out of food, came running back to Geraldine hoping she would share more cheese with them.

Geraldine did not know what to do. Her music mouse was made of cheese and her friends were hungry and wanted to eat the sculpture.

What a hard decision to make! Huk exclaimed. So, what happened?

Geraldine did not know how to explain why she didn't want her friends eating the sculpture, Tuk continued, so she simply blurted out, because it's music!

What's music? her friends asked. Geraldine was again unable to explain.

But then she thought of something. Geraldine took her tail and held it to her lips. She started to blow on her tail. Nothing but noise — not music — came from her efforts, and her friends started to make fun of her. So, this is music? they jeered.

Geraldine was terribly hurt but decided not to give up.

Slowly, a beautiful sound came from her lips. It *was* music!

Her friends were amazed and decided that they could not ask Geraldine to give them chunks of the music mouse to eat.

But then, to everybody's surprise, Geraldine said, since the music is now in me, you can take as much cheese as you want.

Geraldine kept on playing her tail flute while her friends nibbled away at the Parmesan cheese.

That's how she became a musician, Tuk said. Isn't that interesting?

Very, said Huk, and in this tale too, something came out of nothing. Music came out of the mouse's tail — her actual tail. The tail became a flute. That doesn't just happen.

A tale came out of a tail, Tuk mused.

In all these dream tales, something new was created —something larger and more beautiful and more exciting.

But it didn't just happen, Huk decided. It took courage. Tillie needed courage to dig a tunnel under the wall in the dark, not knowing where she'd end up. And Cornelius needed courage to not be afraid of looking like a fool trying to do impossible tricks — impossible for a young croc, that is.

And, Tuk added, we found out that it takes courage to be vulnerable within a friendship and

by Marcos Maldonado

fight for it. That play or dream — or whatever it was — showed us that you can lose a deep friendship if you take it for granted.

That's right. And what about Frederick? To continue to do what he was doing while others thought he was doing nothing at all and kind of scorned him for not helping to gather food for the winter, Huk continued, that couldn't have been easy. And it took courage for Matthew to dream big and dare to become a painter.

I think, Tuk said, that they all needed courage to be creative. Geraldine also looked foolish when she tried to make music with her tail. They all needed the courage to go against others — their family and friends even — who didn't understand or appreciate what they were doing, and the courage to persist when they failed. They needed courage to go it alone. Because they alone could see something most others could not.

So why are we in need of dreams? Huk asked. Do dreams give us courage?

Yes, Tuk replied. Dreams give us the courage to take risks and to persist and to not be afraid but rather inspired to go beyond what is familiar and venture into worlds created by our imagination. Dreams help us come *alive!*

That makes sense, Tuk said. And tales — or tails, as we knew them — connect us to these wonderful worlds we can see with our imagination, our mind's eye, and connect us to the mystery we call life.

Chapter 4

Why We Are in Need of Making Choices with Our Eyes Wide Open

Introduction

Huk and Tuk discover that telling each other tales —
or stories — helps us communicate our thoughts and
feelings to better understand the world we live in.

And so, they share tales with each other and
discover some of the philosophical treasures of
life that are hidden within them. They discuss big
questions like ...

How do I know whether something is truly mine or not?

What does it mean to belong to something?

What is so precious about friendship?

*How do you explain something to someone who
doesn't have the experience to understand your world?*

How does willpower work?

When they discuss these tales with each other,
Huk and Tuk exchange their ideas, their feelings,
their questions. They don't always agree — and
really, why should they? Huk is not Tuk and Tuk is
not Huk. They are Huk and Tuk.

They learn that tales also transport us to realities
outside of ourselves. I like to think of it as *imagination*

travel. When we share tales, we share our imagination with fellow travelers. In that way, sharing tales is a lot like how sharing tails used to be.

One amazing thing about our imaginations is that our dreams — our dreams that connect us to the world we live in and to each other — become alive in them. By discussing tales, Huk and Tuk learn about how it takes courage to follow those dreams by acting on them.

And in order to act on these dreams — or maybe you'd call them hopes or wishes for life — we have to make choices, and some choices are hard to make.

To make hard choices — any real choices! — we have to keep our eyes wide open. That way we can see what paths our choices might lead us down.

In discussing these next tales with each other, Huk and Tuk gain an understanding of the different choices we make in different situations — and how important choices can be. They decide that it's not always clear what the right choice is in every situation. There are lots of reasons we make certain choices, and sometimes we make mistakes too.

These tales are all about making choices and how complicated things can get when deciding what to do.

How Making Choices Can Make All the Difference

— Always by Arnold Lobel —

Huk and Tuk were out for a walk, gazing at the beautiful world around them — a world teeming with life.

See them? Huk pointed to some butterflies fluttering about.

Yes, Tuk replied, I do. Why?

Did you know those three butterflies do the same thing — the *exact* same thing — every day? Huk asked.

Why do they do the same thing every day? Tuk wanted to know.

They say they like it that way, Huk replied.

Don't they get bored? asked Tuk.

I don't think so, said Huk.

The story goes, Huk continued, that one day our friend Grasshopper, who is always on his way somewhere, got a bit tired of walking and decided to sit down on a mushroom on the edge of the road. But right then, these three butterflies flew down and told him to move.

by Anthony Ceron

It turns out that these butterflies had a routine. All three would sit down on this mushroom together for a while *every day*.

But Grasshopper was sitting on that mushroom. Couldn't the butterflies go sit somewhere else? Tuk asked.

Apparently not, Huk said, because, as they told Grasshopper, they *always* sit on *this* mushroom at *this* time. So, Grasshopper — you know how Grasshopper is — decided to get up so the butterflies could sit there.

Once they were comfortably seated on their mushroom, the butterflies continued to tell Grasshopper that they do the exact same thing every day at the same time. *Always!*

Oh no! said Tuk.

Oh yes! said Huk, and they explained to Grasshopper that they like it that way. They wake up every morning, scratch their heads three times — *always*. Open and close their wings four times — *always*. Fly in a circle six times — always. On and on — *always*. After lunch, they sit on the same sunflower and take the same nap —

always. And they have the same dream about sitting on the sunflower taking a nap—

Okay, said Tuk before Huk could say *always* one more time. I get it. So how does this tale end?

Well, said Huk, the butterflies wanted Grasshopper to join their daily routine. They told him that they wanted to meet him every day and tell him about their scratching and flying while sitting on this mushroom they *always* sit on. And they decided that Grasshopper would listen to them the same way he listened to them that day.

But that's when Grasshopper decided that no, he wasn't going to do the same thing every day and that he would be moving on. Because he, Grasshopper told them, does something *different* every day — *always.*

I wonder, said Tuk, did the butterflies *decide* or *choose* to do the same thing every day, or did they simply *do* the same thing every day?

Good question, Tuk! We'll have to think about that one, said Huk.

Tuk didn't have to think very long.

Tuk's eyes lit up. Huk, Tuk said, you know the tale of Sisyphus, right?

I don't think so, Huk replied.

I'll tell you what I remember, Tuk continued. Sisyphus was the king of a big Greek city back when there were gods and goddesses of everything everywhere. He was cunning and managed to cheat death twice.

What! Huk exclaimed. How?

Once he cheated death by chaining up the guy in charge of death — that was Thanatos, Tuk added. But when he did that, no one died anymore. The second time, he persuaded Hades's wife, Persephone, who lives in the underworld — the world of death — to let him go back to his city. So, Zeus, the lightning bolt–throwing god of the universe, decided to punish King Sisyphus.

What was his punishment? Huk asked.

It can get pretty ugly, Huk thought, when the gods decide to punish someone.

Zeus made Sisyphus roll a boulder up a hill, Tuk replied.

Oh! Huk was relieved.

Then Huk asked, What's the big deal? Wasn't Sisyphus able to get the boulder up the hill?

The thing was, said Tuk, once Sisyphus got the boulder up the hill, it would roll back down again. And then he had to roll the boulder back up the hill.

And again and again and again and again, Tuk explained. Over and over for all eternity. That means *always*, forever.

That sounds awful, Huk said.

Tuk agreed. I learned about Sisyphus, Tuk admitted, by reading a book by a French philosopher. He wrote about the absurdity of life and said that we are always trying to find meaning in a meaningless existence.

Like rolling a boulder up a hill until the end of time, Huk concluded.

But then Huk looked confused. How can our *life* be meaningless?

Well, Tuk replied, Camus — that was the philosopher's name: Albert Camus — seemed to think we are all like Sisyphus in life, just rolling a boulder up a hill and watching it roll down again and going back to the bottom to push it up again and again and again. But he also said that if we can *accept* this fact, we can actually be happy. Imagine that!

Huk looked even more puzzled and confused. Can you be happy doing the same thing *always* like the butterflies, or pushing a boulder up a hill *always?* What is there to be happy about?

Well, Tuk mused, maybe, just maybe, if you *decide* — and you make it your *choice* — to push the boulder back up every time, or if you *decide* to sit on the same mushroom every day, it feels different. I mean, since you *decided* it, maybe that's what makes you feel happy.

If you just go along with things, you must feel so powerless, like you don't have a say in what's happening to you in your life at all, Huk said, continuing Tuk's thought. If you *decide* something, you have a say, a say in how you are going to act, even if nothing changes — even if you are going to sit on that same mushroom or push a boulder up a hill. It's your choice now and nobody else's. So yeah, that can make you feel good, or happy, I guess.

Do you think, Huk continued, Sisyphus ended up tricking Zeus again by being happy about his senseless plight, instead of being plain miserable like Zeus had hoped he'd be? Imagine, Huk said, could it be that Sisyphus outsmarted the gods a *third* time?

Yeah, Huk, you might be right, Tuk said, laughing.

Then Tuk continued, Do you think that what matters isn't whether you always do the same thing or always something different, but that you *decide* what you do?

Huk considered this for a minute while looking at the butterflies. Huh, Huk said. I think you might be on to something. It sounds like making our own decisions can be a pretty powerful thing. I never thought of it that way before.

How Making Choices Can Lead to Different Outcomes

— *Alone* by Arnold Lobel —

After their morning walk, Huk and Tuk headed back to Huk's house still laughing about those silly butterflies.

Tuk then felt inspired to tell a story. Here's a tale about Frog and Toad that you might know about, Tuk said.

As you know, Frog and Toad are the best of friends, and they do many things together, just like we do. They have adventures together too and share their experiences. And, what's more, they don't always have the same experiences of the same adventure.

What Tuk said made sense, too, because just like Huk is not Tuk and Tuk is not Huk, Frog is not Toad and Toad is not Frog; they're Frog *and* Toad.

Here's a tale, Tuk continued, where Frog and Toad have a totally different experience of what happened that one day. That day, Toad went over to Frog's house, and, to his utter surprise, he found a note on the door that said, *Dear Toad, I am not at home. I went out. I want to be alone.*

Toad couldn't believe it. Alone? he said. But Frog has me for a friend. Why does he want to be alone?

Huk, feeling somewhat anxious, interrupted Tuk's story, How would you feel if I left *you* a note like that?

I would be worried, too, Tuk admitted. Why would you want to be alone when you have me as a friend? Why would you suddenly decide to do something on your own?

Then Tuk remembered something. Hey, Huk, remember all those stories about dreams and imagination? All those individuals wanted to do things on their own, too, and their friends and family couldn't figure out why.

Yeah, said Huk. But why do we often think of someone going off on their own as something to worry about?

Well, Tuk replied slowly, maybe because, like the butterflies, we learn to expect certain things to stay the same, but then when one person — or butterfly or frog — chooses to do something different one day, we get worried, just like Toad did.

Everywhere Toad looked, Tuk continued — through the windows, in the garden, down Pebble Path — Frog was not there.

So, Toad went to the woods, the meadow and, finally, down to the river. Toad spotted Frog sitting by himself on a small island.

Toad did not think twice — maybe he should have — and decided that Frog must be very sad and that he should cheer him up.

He went home and put together a lunch with yummy sandwiches and a pitcher of cold iced tea. That should make him feel better, Toad thought. And Toad put everything in a basket.

When he got back to the river, he shouted, Frog, it's me, your best friend!

But Frog could not hear him. He was far too far away. Toad decided to take off his jacket. He waved it in the air, but it was no use.

What happened then? Huk asked.

by Diego Frayre

A turtle swam by, Tuk replied. So Toad decided to ask the turtle to bring him to the island where Frog was.

Frog wants to be alone, Toad told the turtle.

So why don't you leave him alone then? the turtle blurted out. Toad agreed and decided that maybe Frog wanted to be alone because he didn't want him as a friend anymore.

Toad got so carried away and cried out to Frog, I'm so sorry for all the dumb things I do and all the silly things I say. Will you *please* be my friend again? Then Toad fell off the turtle and into the river, basket and all.

Frog saw all the commotion and helped Toad onto the island. Toad explained that he had made the lunch to cheer Frog up but now the sandwiches were wet — yak! — and the pitcher was empty.

But I *am* happy, Frog said. I am happy because the sun was shining this morning and because I am a frog and because I have you as my best friend. I just wanted to be by myself and think about how wonderful everything is.

by Isaac Hernandez

Toad felt rather embarrassed and shyly said to Frog, I guess that's a very good reason to want to be alone.

Do you think he was convinced, Tuk? Huk asked.

I think so, said Tuk, but first he had to unconvince himself that Frog wanted nothing to do with him — to not even be his friend anymore.

Frog then told Toad that he was happy to not be alone now, and Frog and Toad ate the wet sandwiches and felt very happy being alone together.

How can they be alone and together? Huk asked.

Well, said Tuk, I think it's like when you and I sit quietly together gazing at the world around us. We're alone *and* we're together.

But why do we think something is wrong when someone chooses to do something on their own? Huk wanted to know.

Maybe Toad thought something was wrong because Frog did not include him in his decision to want to be alone. I mean, Tuk said, if Frog had decided to tell Toad — not just left him a note — Toad might not have been so worried.

Perhaps, Huk said. But do you know what else I think? I think Frog must feel really good that he has a friend like Toad who wanted to make sure his best friend was happy and brought him a delicious lunch — before it all fell into the river, I mean.

Tuk agreed, Toad is a really good friend. Then Tuk laughed and added, When they were alone together, they reconnected their tails. I know frogs and toads don't have tails, but you know what I mean.

I do, responded Huk.

How We Sometimes Choose to Change Our Minds

— The Missing Piece by Shel Silverstein —

Both Huk and Tuk felt hungry after the tale about Frog and Toad, so they started to prepare lunch together.

They made toasted sandwiches of thinly sliced hard-boiled eggs with salt and pepper, and some cherry tomatoes on the side. For dessert, they had some delicious fresh figs.

Tuk was still reflecting on the tale about Frog and Toad. I think, Tuk said, that Toad was afraid something was missing in their friendship and, suddenly feeling alone, got really worried. But in the end, nothing was missing, and he realized he was not at all alone.

Yeah, Huk said, sometimes we can feel like something's missing when it isn't. It can happen in relationships, but it can also happen in ourselves. It can feel like we're not whole, you know?

I heard a tale about a something who felt like they were missing a piece and went on a quest to find it.

Did they find it? Tuk asked while munching on some of the cherry tomatoes.

Well, guess what? Huk continued, On their journey, they actually found out they were not missing anything.

Huh? Tuk said, confused about where Huk was going with this.

Let me explain, said Huk. This something looked like a circle with a piece cut out of it, kind of like a pie missing a slice.

Oh yum, pie! Tuk said.

Huk looked over at Tuk's smiling face, then continued telling the story. Anyway, Huk said, let's call the pie-like something Sandy. In the tale, she doesn't have a name, but I think it'll be easier for me to tell the tale if we give her a name.

So, Sandy decided to go looking for her missing piece. She rolled along looking for it, and she sang a missing-piece song.

On her way, she got hot in the sun and wet in the rain and cold in the snow. Because of her missing piece, she could not roll very fast, so she had time to talk to a worm, to smell a flower and to watch a beetle as she rolled past. She went over oceans and through swamps and up and down mountains, until one day, when she stopped because she thought she had found her missing piece.

But the piece called out to her and said he was not her missing piece, because he was nobody's piece. He was his own piece.

Sandy felt a bit foolish. She apologized and rolled on.

As she rolled, she kept finding all kinds of pieces, but they were all too small or too big, too this or too that. But she didn't give up. Sandy continued on. She had all kinds of adventures on her journey — she fell into holes, and she bumped into walls.

Finally, Sandy *did* find a piece that seemed to fit. And she tried it on, and it *did* fit. It fit perfectly — at last.

That's great, said Tuk. Sandy could go home feeling whole now.

You might think so, said Huk, but actually, the interesting part comes next, because now that Sandy had her missing piece, she ended up rolling faster and faster

by Isaac Hernandez

than ever before. Too fast, in fact. And because she was rolling so very fast, she could not talk to a worm or smell a flower or watch a beetle. And when she wanted to sing her missing-piece song, she could not utter the words right. They got all garbled up.

She became terribly unhappy. Sandy then opened her eyes wide and changed her mind. She decided to go through life without her missing piece and to go back to the way things were. She put the missing piece down and rolled away, singing her missing-piece song as before. Along her journey, she rolled slowly enough to talk to a worm and smell a flower and enjoy watching a beetle as before. And she felt so happy.

Wow, Tuk said. I'm surprised Sandy would decide to give up the piece she spent all that time looking for.

I think Sandy might have actually felt more whole without the missing piece, Huk replied.

Do you think the story is saying you're more complete when you're not complete? Tuk asked.

That sounds very philosophical, Huk said, laughing. But I think that might be it. Sandy was more complete when she rolled slowly so she could talk to the worm and smell the flower, watch the beetle and sing her song. She felt more whole without her missing piece because she felt *connected* to everything around her again, as she did when she set out on her journey to find her missing piece.

So, she was whole all along but didn't realize it? Tuk asked. I guess this adventure opened her eyes and made her realize that it is much more gratifying to move slowly and to feel connected to the world of worms and flowers and beetles around you than to rush by quickly on your own.

How Certain Choices Can Hurt Others

— The Giving Tree by Shel Silverstein —

Huk and Tuk contemplated how being incomplete made you more complete or whole — as in the pie-like something's case — because it gave you the chance to connect to the world around you.

Sandy realized that being complete made it harder to live the way she wanted to, Tuk said. And that tale had a happy ending, but I know a sad tale about how the feeling of missing something never ends and looking for more and more "missing pieces" never made the boy in the tale happy.

Will you tell it to me? Huk asked.

The thing is, Huk, the tale starts off really nice and warm, Tuk said, but then it becomes colder and colder. Do you think you still want me to tell it?

How about we sit by the fireplace to comfort ourselves while you tell this sad, cold tale? Huk suggested. The warmth of the fire should help.

They huddled close to the fire.

Once upon a time, Tuk began, there was a tree and there was a little boy.

The little boy loved visiting the tree often. He would make a crown out of her leaves and pretend he was a king. He would climb up her trunk, swing from her branches and eat her apples.

The tree loved the boy. The boy loved the tree. The tree was happy. The boy was happy.

As the boy grew older, he stopped coming to visit every day. And the tree was often alone.

After a long while, the boy returned, and the tree invited him to climb up her trunk, eat her apples and be happy like before. But this time the boy, older now, said he was too old to climb and play.

Instead, the boy asked the tree, can you give me money?

I can't, the tree replied, but you can take my apples and sell them in the city so that you'll have money and be happy.

by Diego Frayre

And the boy did just that. He shook all the apples out of the tree and carried them away. The tree was happy she could help.

Was the boy happy? Huk asked.

I don't know, Tuk said. Maybe ... but I don't think they were happy *together* as they used to be, like Frog and Toad are or like we are. Their relationship changed and it wasn't what it was before.

After the boy took all the apples, Tuk continued, he didn't come back to visit for a very long time.

And the tree was alone for a very long time, Huk interjected.

That's right, Tuk said, so when the boy returned, the tree shook with joy! It had been such a long time since she had last seen him. She invited him again to climb up her trunk and swing from her branches. But the boy only said that he was too busy now. He wanted a house to keep him warm. He wanted a family.

Can you give me a house? he asked her.

No, she replied, but you may cut off my branches and build a house. Then you will be happy.

by Roger Gutierrez

So, Tuk continued, the boy cut off all her branches so he could build his house. The tree was happy.

What! Huk interrupted. Do you *really* think the tree was happy? Helping the *boy* out made her happy, but what I mean is, was *she* happy?

The boy never did anything to make her happy, that's clear, Tuk replied. When he was a boy, he came every day to see her and be with her. But when he grew up, he just visited her when he wanted things. The relationship was taking a turn for the worse, if you ask me, Tuk said, because the boy was no longer connected to the tree — he just wanted things from her.

I don't like the boy, Huk blurted out. He's taking the tree for granted. He could have visited her with his family and his kids, who could climb up her trunk and swing from her branches.

I don't like the boy either, Tuk said. He doesn't seem to appreciate all she's doing to make him happy.

I wonder why the tree loves the boy so much, Huk said.

That's hard to say, Tuk said. Maybe it's important for the tree to see the boy happy no matter what.

So how does this sad tale end? Huk asked.

Well, said Tuk, the next time the boy left, he stayed away for even longer than ever before. By the time he did show up, he was old and tired. He asked the tree for a boat to sail away with.

Did she give him the boat? Huk asked.

Of course, Tuk said, in a way. The tree let the boy — or, I guess he was a man now — cut down her trunk so he could make a boat and sail away.

Huk moved closer to the fire and said, That's so sad. The boy sounds like he's looking for all sorts of things — all sorts of missing pieces — to make him happy. But he's never really happy, ever.

Why do you think he kept coming back? Huk asked.

I don't really know, Tuk said. Maybe because he knew she loved him and that she would do anything to make him happy. She seemed happy every time she gave him something of her tree.

I think he's a sourpuss, Huk decided. He's never really happy or grateful.

In the end, Tuk said, the boy came back one more time. And when he returned, the tree told him she had nothing left to give.

by Brettany Villalobos

I'm just an old stump, she said. And the boy replied, I don't need very much now, maybe just a quiet place to sit and rest.

Well then, the tree said, come sit and rest. Stumps are good for sitting on and resting. And the boy did. And the tree was happy.

But the tree is dead now! Huk cried out. She can't grow back a trunk and branches and apples...

Yes, the tree is dead now, said Tuk. That's why it's a very sad story, I think. And it's a tale about how the boy took the tree and her love for him for granted.

The fire in Huk's fireplace was slowly going out, and Huk and Tuk were feeling very sad together.

Then Tuk said, It's like when we just take the world for granted and use up everything the Earth gives us and think little of it because we figure that's what the Earth is for. Just like the boy thought the tree was there to give him want he wanted and needed. It's about time we opened our eyes wide and made some real choices about how we treat the world instead.

When we all still had tails that connected us, Huk said, nobody acted the way that boy did. We felt connected to everything and we made decisions with our eyes wide open about how to treat the Earth, because we realized our choices affected others too.

And the tree can't give anymore when she's dead, Huk said, no matter how much she loves the boy.

I know, said Tuk, that's why this is such a sad tale.

How Making Choices Can Inspire Others

— Tico and the Golden Wings by Leo Lionni *—*

Tuk stayed over at Huk's house that night. Thankfully, by the time they got up in the morning, the sun was shining, and they both felt happy again.

Every day *is* a new day.

At breakfast, they sat sipping their hot tea and eating their berries and fruits and cinnamon toast.

Tuk looked thoughtful and then said, Huk, I know another tale about giving. It's about a bird named Tico who gives all his golden feathers away. This tale has a good ending.

Oh great, said Huk, we could use some cheering up.

In the tale, Tico starts by telling us about himself, Tuk said. He's not sure how it happened, but he says he was born with no wings. He sang and hopped around like the other birds, but he couldn't fly. Luckily, his friends loved him and brought him berries and fruits and took good care of him.

175

But Tico was sad that he could not fly. He would ask, Why can't I soar through the sky like the others? And he would wish for golden wings so he could fly high over the mountaintops.

Then one night, Tuk continued, Tico was awakened by a peculiar sound. He opened his eyes and saw a wishing bird. The wishing bird told him to make a wish and promised that it would come true.

Tico told the wishing bird about his dream of having golden wings. Then a flash of light appeared, and the wishing bird vanished in the deep dark sky.

His wish had come true: Tico had a pair of golden wings.

Tico wasn't sure if this could be real, so he slowly opened his wings and cautiously started to fly. When he felt the wind beneath his wings, Tico flew over flower patches and saw a river below that looked like a silver necklace. Oh, the world was mesmerizing!

But when he flew back to be with his friends, they said things like, Now you think you're better than us with your golden wings?

And they jeered at him, You always wanted to be different.

by Kairi Pacheco

by Kaelie Lopez

Then they all flew away.

After his friends left, Tuk continued, Tico started to feel very lonely. Although he had beautiful golden wings and could fly like his friends now, they had all left him.

Huk said thoughtfully, Life is hard without friends.

But were they really his friends? Tuk wondered. Would friends just fly away and leave you all by yourself like that?

They also accused Tico of wanting to be different, Huk said.

But he was also different from them when he had *no* wings, Tuk said, and they cared for him then. They took care of him by bringing him fruits and berries.

So, what changed? Huk wanted to know. Were they jealous now that he had golden wings?

For a minute, Huk was lost in thought.

Then Huk looked at Tuk and said, You know, being different can be a good thing or a bad thing, just like being alone can be a good thing or a bad thing. And being complete can mean being incomplete sometimes. Things seem to always be kind of complicated that way.

Tuk agreed that life is a lot more complicated but didn't know what to say because it is so complicated.

Tuk continued with the tale instead. While Tico sat all alone and felt miserable, his eyes suddenly opened wide, and he spotted a basket maker who had many baskets lying all around him. Tico noticed that the basket maker was crying.

Why are you sad? Tico asked the basket maker. The basket maker told him that his child was very sick, and he didn't have the money to buy the medicine his child needed. He was too poor.

Then Tico thought about how he could help. He decided to give the basket maker one of his golden feathers.

The basket maker was grateful and thanked Tico for saving his child's life.

That's so sweet, Huk said. Tico must have felt happy knowing that he'd helped the basket maker and his child.

He did, Tuk said. But look, suddenly something else happened. There was now a beautiful silk black feather where the golden feather had been.

Tico started giving his golden feathers to people who needed help. He gave new puppets to a poor puppeteer, a spinning wheel to help an old woman make a shawl and a compass to help guide a lost fisherman. After Tico had given away his last golden feather, his wings were as black as India ink.

At least Tico still had wings to fly, Huk said. I like that about this story. It's not like the tale about the giving tree who gave and gave until she had nothing left.

I know another way it's not like that tale, said Tuk. The tree gave everything to a boy who only wanted more, but Tico gave to people who really needed — not just *wanted* — the things Tico gave.

Exactly! said Huk. And another really important way it's different is that those people Tico helped out were all so happy and so grateful, not like that sourpuss boy.

by Abraham Roman

Did Tico go back to his friends? Huk wanted to know.

Yes, Tuk said, he wanted to be with his friends again, but he was worried they might not welcome him back. But they were all happy when they saw him and said, Now you are just like us.

Tico and his friends huddled together, and Tico was so happy, he couldn't sleep. He happily thought of all the things he had done while he was away from his friends and realized that even though his feathers were black like his friends' feathers, he wasn't just like his friends. He'd had lots of different experiences they did not have.

That's true, Huk said, then added, Tico was different now in another way, too. His sort-of friends had no idea what he had done with his golden feathers. They simply liked that he now looked just like them.

I think, Tuk concluded, that when Tico's eyes were wide open, he connected to the world around him and to the people he saw who needed help. He was able to see that they were in need, and that's when he decided to help them.

It seems that his friends had their eyes half closed, Tuk added, since they only saw that Tico now looked like them with his black wings. And it seems that's all that mattered to them.

But you forget, Huk said, they did help him when he didn't have any wings at all, remember?

True, Tuk admitted, but when he had golden wings, they figured he felt like he was better than them, and they just flew off, leaving him alone. I mean, they didn't see Tico as a threat when he had no wings, is my point.

Well, Huk concluded, I guess they reconnected in some way. His friends were happy he looked like them and Tico was happy to not be alone.

How Making Hard Choices Is Never Easy

— *Doctor De Soto* by William Steig —

After Huk and Tuk finished their breakfast, they decided to go out for a stroll. They walked through the meadow covered in wildflowers and along the creek with tall grass rising from its banks. While they walked, they could hear birds chirping in the woods nearby. It was a peaceful morning, and the air was fresh and cool.

As they approached Tuk's home, they passed the crumbling wall where a mouse family lived.

You know, said Huk, as a mouse scurried by, I know a tale about a mouse dentist. Isn't that funny?

The mouse was named Doctor De Soto, said Huk. He was the only dentist — I think — in his small town, and his wife, Mrs. De Soto, was his assistant. Doctor De Soto had been the town dentist for many years. He helped the large animals as well as the smaller animals, but he refused to help animals that were dangerous to mice. The shingle outside his office said as much. It read:

Cats and Other Dangerous Animals
Not Accepted for Treatment

One day, as the De Sotos took a break and looked out the window, they saw a well-dressed fox with a bandana tied around his jaw.

Doctor De Soto quickly assessed the situation and called out the window, I cannot treat you, sir. Haven't you read my sign?

But the fox wept so bitterly and seemed to be in so much pain. Please, he wailed, have mercy. I am suffering.

Doctor De Soto and his wife were troubled. Should they let him in or not? A fox is dangerous to mice. That was obvious. But the fox was in terrible pain. That too was obvious.

Would you let him in if you were the De Sotos? Tuk interrupted Huk's telling of the tale. I mean, you would want to help someone who's in terrible pain, but what if your life were on the line? That's serious. That seems like an impossible decision to have to make.

I don't know, said Huk. How do you even begin to decide something like that?

I'm not sure, said Tuk. Doctor De Soto's job was to help those who need help and so it makes sense that he would want to honor his commitment to helping others.

I know, Huk replied, but I think he also didn't want to end up like the giving tree — dead! And that's why his sign says specifically that he won't help those dangerous to him and his wife.

Even though he's the only dentist in town who can help those in need? Tuk continued. That's a really hard decision to make, you know.

So, what does the story say? Tuk asked, hoping to avoid the question altogether.

Well, as the story goes, Huk said, Mrs. De Soto *did* know what to do. She decided they should risk it. She pushed the buzzer to let the fox in.

The fox was up the stairs in no time. He fell to his knees and cried, My tooth is killing me. Please, please do something. I beg you.

Doctor De Soto went straight to work. Please remove the bandana, sir, he said, and have a seat on the floor over here.

Remember, Doctor De Soto is a mouse, Huk continued, so he needed to climb up a ladder to reach the fox's mouth. Open wide, he said, and he climbed into the fox's mouth, which was not at all a comfortable place for any mouse to be.

Doctor De Soto discovered the problem immediately. The fox had a thoroughly rotten molar and terribly bad breath. He told the fox that the tooth would have to come out. But he promised to make the fox a new tooth to replace it.

The fox agreed. Just make the pain go away, he wailed. But a fox is still a fox, and he could not help thinking how delicious the De Sotos would be to eat. The thought alone made his jaw quiver.

Keep open! Doctor De Soto yelled.

I think Doctor De Soto is terribly brave, Tuk said. I don't think I would have had the nerve to do what that mouse did. Imagine! Entering the fox's mouth? That's unbelievable!

I know, said Huk, just telling the tale makes me nervous. So then, Huk continued, Doctor De Soto, with the help of his wife, gave the fox some gas so he would not feel anything when they yanked the tooth out.

Soon the fox was in dreamland. And in his dream, he mumbled, Mmm, yummy, raw with a pinch of salt, and a dry white wine indeed!

by Kairi Pacheco

It was clear what he was dreaming about. The De Sotos quickly placed a pole in the fox's mouth to make sure it stayed wide open. Then they fastened the extractor to the bad tooth and turned the winch. And the rotten molar came out!

When the fox came to, Doctor De Soto told him to return the next day so he could put the new tooth in its place. Be here at eleven sharp, he told the fox.

Still somewhat dizzy from the gas, the fox went back home. But on the way, he couldn't help thinking — after all, he is a fox — whether it would be in bad taste (no pun intended, Huk said and giggled) to eat the De Sotos after the job was done.

Back at the dentist's office, Doctor De Soto muttered, Raw with salt indeed! How foolish we were to trust a fox. It's like we didn't even read our own sign out front stating *clearly* that animals dangerous to mice would not be accepted for treatment.

Mrs. De Soto, on the other hand, thought the fox would not harm them. After all, they were helping him.

You don't understand, Doctor De Soto said, a fox is a fox. What do you expect? He doesn't choose to be a fox. A fox is a fox is a fox and that's that. He can't choose not to be one.

That night they lay in bed worrying and wondering whether they should let the fox in the next day. They had already helped the fox by pulling his rotten tooth. Should they do more than that?

Would you let the fox in a second time? Tuk asked Huk.

Ha! Huk exclaimed, now thoroughly convinced. I would not even have allowed him in in the first place. And you?

Tuk didn't want to appear as scared as Huk seemed to be, and nonchalantly said, Well, I'd have to think about that.

So, Huk continued, Doctor De Soto made it clear that once he started a job, he always finished it. He was determined to let the fox back in the next day at eleven o'clock sharp.

A very cheerful fox showed up the next morning.

The fox was thrilled. The gold tooth was beautiful. Doctor De Soto set it in the socket and hooked it up to the teeth on both sides.

The fox figured he really shouldn't eat the De Sotos, but how could he resist? Did he have a choice in the matter? That was the question.

Then, before letting the fox go, Doctor De Soto explained that they were not quite finished and that he and his wife had recently developed a remarkable ointment that would prevent any toothaches in the future.

The De Sotos expected the news to sound like music to the fox's big ears. And it did! The fox was delighted and was eager to try the ointment.

In the meantime, the fox had made up his mind to eat the De Sotos with the help of his brand-new tooth.

Why are foxes so mean? Tuk asked. The De Sotos helped him. Isn't that something for the fox to consider, Tuk asked, and at least *try* to resist eating them?

Are foxes mean? Huk responded. Or is it simply their nature to eat mice?

Mean or not mean, it's just not right. So then what? Tuk wanted to know, worried that the fox was going to eat the De Sotos.

So, Doctor De Soto carefully applied the ointment on all the fox's teeth.

The fox looked extremely happy. He was enjoying the best of all worlds — no more pain, an ointment that would prevent toothaches forever and, last but not least, a delicious delicacy before leaving the dentist's office.

Then Doctor De Soto told the fox to close his jaws tight and to keep them closed for a minute so the ointment could penetrate the dentine.

When the fox tried to open his mouth, however, his teeth were stuck together.

Oh my, Doctor De Soto said, excuse me, I forgot to tell you that you will not be able to open your mouth for a day or two in order for the ointment to really work. But not to worry, no toothaches ever again!

And while Doctor De Soto and his wife smiled at him, all the fox could say was, Frank oo berry mush, as he stumbled down the stairs, stunned at what had just happened.

And so, Huk concluded, Doctor De Soto and his wife had outfoxed the fox.

That's a great tale, Tuk said. But I have a question for you. The De Sotos chose to lie, right? Is that okay?

Well, said Huk, I guess it depends. Maybe lying is not the *right* thing to do, but it may be the *necessary* thing to do in some cases, like this one. They chose the necessary thing to do over the right thing to do.

I think this tale is about hard choices, Huk continued. The De Sotos had to decide, or choose, to let the fox in — twice — and then they had to make the choice to lie about the so-called ointment to prevent toothaches in order to protect their lives.

And look, Huk went on, they helped the fox out of his misery. They didn't have to do that. And they gave him a brand-new gold tooth. They didn't have to do that either.

Given what they were willing to do for him, they then had to do what they needed to do to save their own lives from a fox who was ready to eat them.

It was clear that the fox had no intention of sparing their little lives, Tuk said. He didn't even try to resist the urge to eat them after they had helped him out. They could have let him go on suffering with his bad tooth.

That's what I don't like, Tuk continued. I get it, he's a fox, but I think he's a mean fox because he doesn't even consider the fate of the De Sotos. And what's more important, lying about some ointment or saving your life from a mean fox?

Huk had to admit that saving your life was definitely more important.

Both Huk and Tuk were truly impressed with the De Sotos' courage. They must have been afraid to let the fox in and treat him the way they would any other patient. And so, they also took responsibility for lying to the fox in order to save their own lives.

Well, Huk mused, they saved their own lives, but if in fact Doctor De Soto was the only dentist in town, who would all the animals go to when they had dental problems if the fox had eaten the De Sotos? So, this fox is selfish, too, because he expects to be helped with *his* toothache but doesn't care that if he eats the De Sotos, the other animals have nobody to go to when they have tooth pain.

Well, Tuk concluded. They saved their own lives by keeping their eyes wide open when deciding how best to help this mean fox out of his misery and keep themselves safe at the same time. Those are the hardest decisions to make. Of course, it would have been easier to just decide not to help him or be foolish in thinking the fox would never harm them because they helped him. Making hard choices is really complicated.

You know, Huk said, come to think of it, when we had tails and were connected to the world and others around us, we were very careful about our decisions because we knew how they would affect others. When we lost our tails, we became less mindful and often made decisions that were bad for the world and others around us. It's as though we've been living with our eyes half closed, like the boy who never even considered the tree in his decisions and always wanted more from her.

And, said Tuk, continuing Huk's thought, since we didn't feel connected, we felt we had all these missing pieces and started looking for them. But these missing pieces never made us feel connected in the way we did when we had our tails. And ... in trying to find all these missing pieces, we started to take the world for granted.

Hmm, Huk mused, when we feel connected to the world and others around us, we don't even think of ourselves as being incomplete and having missing pieces.

I like that, Tuk said, then added, To be connected, we have to keep our eyes wide open, like Sandy and Tico and the De Sotos. And then we can make good decisions too.

Huk started to laugh. I think philosophy, as an art, said Huk, is really the art of keeping our eyes wide open.

I think so too, Tuk agreed.

Chapter 5

How to Deal with What Is Beyond Our Control

Introduction

Huk and Tuk discover that telling each other tales can help us reconnect to the mystery called life. They learn that telling tales brings back a sense of wonder — and it is this sense of wonder that helps us reconnect with each other and to the world around us. In the tales Huk and Tuk tell each other, they wonder about what it means to be fair, or to be a friend, or to have willpower. They find out it is also possible to wonder about what is on the other side of a wall — any wall — and to expand their vision using imagination. They find out that wondering, and especially wondering together, helps to keep the spark of life alive — even when life is challenging and there are no clear answers.

They also learn about the importance of dreams and find that dreams, which seem to come out of nowhere, reconnect us by sparking our curiosity and our imagination. Huk and Tuk, of course, also materialized out of nowhere — a very creative place in infinite space; a place that's everywhere and nowhere at the same time.

After learning about dreams, Huk and Tuk tell each other tales about how our decisions can help us make our dreams come true. You may wonder how decisions can possibly do that, though. Well, when we simply follow along and don't think much about why we are doing one thing instead of another thing, we're making decisions with our eyes half closed, really, and may not see the opportunities to make our dreams come true. Huk and Tuk know that we need to keep our eyes wide open when we venture through life, much like we do when we wander through the woods.

Finally, in this chapter, Huk and Tuk discuss how to deal with the things in life that are beyond our control. There are many — so, so many — situations in life that are not in our control, yet we have to deal with them one way or another. But how, and on what basis, do we make our decisions in those situations?

Huk and Tuk discuss what lies at the basis of the decisions we need to make when things are beyond our control. They know that this is a very tough subject and that without some kind of deep connection to the world around us and to each other, it is nearly impossible to deal with these kinds of situations.

What It Means to Be Brave When Faced with What Is Beyond Our Control

— *Dragons and Giants* by Arnold Lobel —

Huk and Tuk sat on Tuk's back porch one afternoon, sipping the apple juice they had made together with the apples from the trees below Huk's house.

You know, said Tuk, tales have a way of making you wiser. Huk and Tuk always enjoyed sharing wonderful, full-of-wonder tales with each other, but this was a new idea to contemplate.

Wiser? asked Huk. How so?

Well, Tuk said, I think tales get you to think about things differently. I think they can even make you think about life differently.

Tales teach us, Tuk continued, that what we think we know, we really don't know.

Kind of like Socrates? Huk asked. Tuk looked puzzled. You know, Socrates, the famous Greek philosopher? He said that too, continued Huk, but I don't think he was talking about how *tales* make you wiser. Anyway, how do tales make us realize that what we think we know, we don't really know?

Well, Tuk began, remember the tale about the missing piece? Remember how we thought the pie-like something — oh, remember how we called her Sandy? — would be delighted when she finally found her missing piece? But then, to our surprise, she ended up putting the missing piece down and continued her life without it. She felt more complete without her missing piece than with it. That makes you think, doesn't it?

That's true, Huk said. I think most of us would have thought that happiness is a result of being perfect or complete, or something like that.

Yeah, Tuk said, but then Sandy learned that life is not about being perfect; it's about relationships, really. After she found her missing piece, Sandy rolled past them so fast that she missed out on talking with the worm, smelling a flower and seeing the butterflies. She had no time for them anymore. So she decided to continue her life without the missing piece — and she felt more perfect without it. See, Sandy first thought she'd be happier *with* the missing piece, but then when she had found it, she learned she was actually much happier without it.

Oh, I get it, said Huk, she learned that what she thought she knew — that she would be happier with her missing piece — she didn't know, and she was actually happier without it.

That's true, Tuk agreed.

I know a tale about Frog and Toad wanting to know whether they were really brave or not, Tuk said. After looking in the mirror and wondering whether they *looked* brave, they decided they would have to find out if they really were brave by *actually* climbing the mountain just outside Toad's house. They wanted to find out what they thought might be true was really true, because Frog and Toad figured out that *thinking* they may be brave and possibly *looking* brave didn't by any means indicate whether they were *in fact* brave.

Or foolish, Huk interrupted. Remember the tale about Doctor De Soto and his wife and the fox? It wasn't clear in that tale whether the De Sotos were *actually* brave by letting the fox into their dentistry or if they were maybe just foolish. Even Doctor De Soto thought it was foolish to have trusted a fox and to have let him in!

Although, Huk continued, the De Sotos *did* realize the danger involved in letting the fox in — twice. It's not that they had their eyes closed. That would have made them foolish, I think. In fact, they had their eyes wide open and decided to help the fox anyway. They helped him because he was in pain, not because he was a fox, an animal that could be very, very dangerous to mice like the De Sotos.

Okay, Tuk replied, that does make sense. So, someone is foolish if they are not aware of the danger involved? But you can't always *be aware* of exactly the danger you are in. There's always something that is beyond your control.

So, what happened to Frog and Toad? Huk wanted to know. Were they aware of any possible danger they would face climbing the mountain? Or was it foolish of them to test their bravery that way?

Well, you tell me, Tuk said.

Frog and Toad started to climb the mountain, Tuk continued. This was going to be their test to prove to themselves whether they were a brave frog and a brave toad or not.

They knew it might be dangerous but did not know what kind of danger they would be in. That was beyond their control.

So, Tuk said, everything was going smoothly as they climbed the mountain. Then they came to a dark cave and — suddenly — a snake came out of the cave and said, Hello lunch. The snake opened his mouth wide.

Oh no! Huk exclaimed. Frog and Toad would make a delicious lunch for that snake.

It's okay, Tuk said. Frog and Toad jumped out of the way *just* in time. Toad was shaking like a leaf and tried to sound brave. He cried out, I'm not afraid!

After that first scare, they continued their journey up the mountain.

It's brave of them to continue climbing the mountain instead of running back home, Huk said.

by Kyeann Ogalino

Tuk nodded and kept going. They climbed on and heard a loud noise and then many large stones came rolling down the mountain.

Toad cried out, It's an avalanche! Frog and Toad jumped out of the way *just* in time.

Frog trembled and tried to sound brave, shouting, I'm not afraid!

They are being tested on this hike up the mountain, Huk said. These are dangerous encounters. Poor Frog and Toad must be scared stiff even though they don't want to admit it, of course, shouting instead that they are not afraid.

Did they go back home after that? Huk asked. I would have!

No, Tuk said, they went *all the way* up to the top of the mountain.

That means they are brave, Huk concluded. I would have called it a day — brave or not — and gone back home.

The tale continues with Frog and Toad suddenly seeing the shadow of a hawk overhead, and they both jumped under a rock *just* in time. The hawk

by Carlos Dominguez

flew away. We're not afraid, they both screamed. And they started running down the mountain as fast as they could. They ran and ran and ran until they finally got to Toad's house.

So, they got home safe? Huk wanted to know.

Yes, and then Toad jumped into his bed and pulled the covers over his head and Frog jumped into the closet and shut the door. And they stayed there for a very long time.

Being scared doesn't mean you're not brave, Huk decided. It means being able to carry on even though you are scared. So then do you have to be somewhat scared in order to be brave?

I think so, Tuk replied, because being scared is being scared of something beyond your control. I mean, Frog and Toad were not in control of the snake, who was looking for lunch, or the avalanche that was coming their way, or the hawk that swooped down.

That's interesting, isn't it? said Huk. I think we often think that being brave means not being scared of something, but that's not it at all.

And, Tuk continued, if Frog and Toad were not afraid at all, they may not have jumped out of the way of the snake, the avalanche or the hawk. They obviously had their eyes wide open to avert the danger they were in and continue their journey up the mountain.

Even though they were really scared, Huk commented, it didn't stop them from going all the way up the mountain. So, in my opinion, Frog and Toad found out they were in fact brave. They were brave in their encounters with what was way out of their control. What do you think?

Tuk agreed, I think Frog and Toad are one brave frog and one brave toad.

by Jessica Leon

How to Deal with the Forces of Nature Beyond Our Control

— *The Garden* by Arnold Lobel —

The next day Tuk went over to Huk's house and, as always, was impressed with how well Huk tended the front garden. Tuk was amazed at the many flowers and shrubs and bushes. Tuk could see that Huk gave the garden a lot of care and attention.

It's rather wild, Tuk thought, but it all looks so perfectly imperfect, or — and Tuk smiled — imperfectly perfect.

Huk came outside to greet Tuk, and together they quietly enjoyed the garden for several minutes.

Huk then asked if Tuk knew the funny story about how his best friend's beautiful garden made Toad want a garden of his own.

Tuk wasn't surprised to hear this, since Tuk had been having similar thoughts about Huk's garden.

Huk started telling the story, it's hard work, Frog told Toad. But here are some seeds. Put these seeds in the ground and that way you can start your garden.

Tuk, not being quite sure how gardens work exactly, asked, What happened next?

Toad took the seeds and ran home. He carefully created a flowerbed the way Frog had shown him and planted the flower seeds.

Then Toad instructed the seeds to grow. Now seeds, Toad said, start growing!

Toad walked up and down the flowerbed, hoping the seeds would start growing, but he didn't see any change.

Did Toad *really* think that the seeds would start growing the minute he put them in the ground? Even Tuk knew that it took more time and patience than that!

Obviously, Toad had no clue, Huk said. Toad then put his head close to the ground and raised his voice, NOW SEEDS, START GROWING!

Alas, said Huk, as you may have expected, the seeds did *not* start to grow. Tuk nodded, trying to demonstrate that he knew that's not how it works.

Toad tried again and raised his voice even more, practically yelling at the seeds to start growing. At this point, Frog, hearing all the noise, went over to Toad's house.

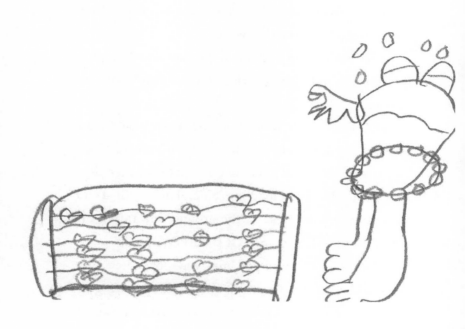

by Samantha Ceballos

What is going on here? Frog asked.

My seeds won't grow, Toad said, sounding exasperated.

They are afraid to grow, said Frog. Leave them alone for a couple of days. Let the sun shine and the rain fall on them. Then they will start to grow.

That night, Toad looked out the window and saw that his seeds still had not started to grow. Then Toad thought, If my seeds are afraid to grow, maybe it's because they're afraid of the dark. So, he took candles out to the garden with him and put them in the ground. He read the seeds a story by candlelight, hoping they would not be afraid.

And so, Huk continued, Toad sang, read poems and played his violin for his seeds.

Tuk interrupted, Toad plays the violin?

I didn't know that either, said Huk and then continued, Eventually Toad got very tired and fell asleep next to his seeds. He slept for a long time.

When Frog showed up to see how Toad was doing, he found his friend fast asleep. Frog nudged Toad awake and said, Look Toad, look at your garden.

 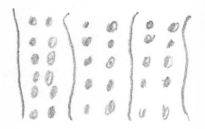

by Roberto Camacho

by Kyeann Ogalino

And guess what, Tuk — tiny shoots had started to come out of the ground!

Toad was overjoyed and said, My seeds stopped being afraid and finally decided to start growing! But Toad also agreed that having a garden was really hard work.

Do you think Toad learned anything about growing a garden?

Well, Tuk replied, Frog did tell Toad growing a garden was hard work. And, I guess, Toad figured that meant *doing* something, like singing to the seeds, and reading poems and playing his violin. See, that's all hard work to Toad.

And sitting around doing nothing — just waiting for the seeds to grow — is not particularly hard work, is it?

Tuk could see how Toad was confused. Waiting for seeds to grow is not hard work, Tuk conceded.

So, what does make it hard work, then? Tuk asked.

We cannot force seeds to grow, said Huk. That's beyond our control. We can create conditions for them to grow, but the seeds do their own growing in their own time.

Maybe Toad learned that to grow a garden is to let *the garden* do the growing. I mean, said Tuk, we cannot do the growing *for* the seeds. That's out of our control.

And, said Huk, we're only now slowly learning that nature has its own way of doing things, after we've thought for so long that we can control it. Well, when we still had tails, because our tails connected us to nature, we knew we had no control over nature, but somehow we forgot it again when we lost our tails.

Tuk laughed and said, So we now have to learn what Toad had to learn — that we cannot control what is beyond our control. Isn't that some profound insight!

Huk laughed and said, Tales do have a way of getting us to see things in a new way — in a way we had not thought of before. Or sometimes, I think they even reveal the obvious and get us to see what was there but had not been considered before.

by Isabella Cervantes

How to Accept Things When They Get Out of Control

— *A New House* by Arnold Lobel —

Below Huk's house are a lot of apple trees. In fall, Huk and Tuk go down there to pick apples to bring home and bake apple pie — *delicious* apple pie.

While they were picking apples one day, Tuk looked up at the trees and asked Huk, Remember our friend Grasshopper? Did you know he ran into a *lot* of trouble one day all because of *an apple?*

What happened? Huk asked.

Grasshopper climbed to the top of a steep hill, Tuk said, and he was quite hungry when he got all the way up there. He spotted a large apple lying on the ground, so he decided to take a big bite out of it.

But Worm lived in that apple and cried out to Grasshopper, Look what you did! Now there is a big hole in my roof.

Oh no! Grasshopper thought. I am so sorry, Grasshopper told Worm. But before he could finish apologizing, the apple started rolling down the hill.

by Fawad Fnu

That sure doesn't sound good, said Huk.

Worm cried out in a panic, Tuk continued, pleading with Grasshopper to stop the apple from rolling down the hill.

Poor Grasshopper ran after the apple, but the apple started rolling faster and faster and Grasshopper could not do anything to stop it.

Grasshopper heard Worm, who was totally upset, cry out, Help! Please!

Worm's head was bumping on the walls! His dishes were falling off the shelf. Everything turned into a complete mess!

Can you imagine? Tuk said. His bathtub was in the living room! His bed was in the kitchen!

The situation only got worse and worse, Tuk continued.

Grasshopper kept running. This situation was way beyond his control. He did not know what else to do to stop the apple from rolling and rolling and rolling. Grasshopper could not catch up.

The apple rolled all the way down the hill. At the bottom of the hill, the apple — namely Worm's

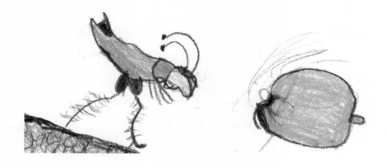

by Abraham Ponce

house — smashed into a tree and was destroyed. Grasshopper wasn't sure what to say, so he blurted out the obvious: Your house is gone!

Worm must have been really angry at Grasshopper, Huk said. Imagine if *your* house had smashed apart.

That's the interesting thing, Tuk replied. I don't think Worm *was* angry. Rather, he appreciated that Grasshopper made a real effort to try and save his house.

Worm knew that after Grasshopper had taken a bite out of the apple, the situation just got way out of control.

And Grasshopper knew that he hadn't meant to hurt Worm. He hadn't destroyed his house on purpose.

Sure, said Huk, that's easy for *you* to say. Whether Grasshopper did this on purpose or not doesn't really matter — Worm's house was wrecked.

That's true, but the tale still has a pretty good ending, Tuk said, because after Worm's house was gone, he climbed up an apple tree in order to get a new house.

The tree was full of apples and Worm could choose which apple would become his new house.

Even before his house was completely destroyed, Worm had mentioned to Grasshopper that he needed a new house because the old house had a hole in the roof. They both laughed at that and felt a little better about the situation.

Things did get way out of hand, Huk said, but Grasshopper did what he could, and Worm realized that. I guess that makes a difference somehow. If Grasshopper had simply ignored what happened after he had taken a bite out of Worm's house, Worm would probably have been really angry.

I would have been furious that my house was destroyed, Tuk said, even if Grasshopper didn't intend to do it.

Hmm, Huk replied, I guess I could be mad or upset, but not at Grasshopper. I mean Grasshopper already feels bad, and Worm didn't want to make him feel any worse.

It's a tough situation, Tuk conceded, I'll give you that. I'm glad Worm found a new house; otherwise, he may not have been so nice to Grasshopper.

I know, Huk agreed. And what's more, if you think about it, something good came out of it too — a new home without a hole in the roof even.

Isn't it interesting, Tuk said, how things that look one way — and in this case it didn't look very good — can turn out yet another way completely! And in this case, they even turned out for the better.

How to Face the Ultimate Loss of Control

— Duck, Death and the Tulip by Wolf Erlbruch —

Huk thought about how sometimes things can happen in life that we never expect to happen and how we usually just go about our daily lives not giving things much thought. For instance, Huk thought, Grasshopper had no idea that eating a bite out of the apple would result in destroying Worm's house.

After Huk shared these thoughts with Tuk, Tuk looked solemnly at Huk and said, And sometimes death is what we least expect.

Huk shuddered. Huk had not thought about death at all.

Shaken by Tuk's remark, Huk said, Actually, I know a beautiful tale about death and how it can come so unexpectedly.

Tuk, have you heard the tale about Duck, Death and the tulip?

No, replied Tuk, but I would like to hear it if it is a beautiful tale, as you say.

232

Well, Huk began, Duck used to live near the pond, close to the apple trees down below my house.

Duck went about her daily life being a duck. One day she suddenly noticed that something was behind her, so she looked around.

She saw someone and asked, Who are you?

I am Death, the someone answered. So you finally noticed me.

Duck, of course, was completely taken off guard and scared stiff. She asked Death whether he was coming to fetch her.

Oh no, Death replied, I'm really always close by. But usually nobody notices me.

So, what happened when Duck realized Death had been close by all along? Tuk asked.

Well, Huk said, Death added that he was always close by — *just in case* — whereupon Duck asked, just in case *what*? I guess Duck was still scared, Huk added, and didn't trust Death at all.

In case something happens to you, Death replied, a nasty cold or an accident.

Are you going to *make* something happen? Duck asked.

And again, Huk said, Death came back with a very interesting answer. First, he responded that he is *always* close by, and then he replied that it is *life* that takes care of that, the coughs and colds and whatever happens to you.

And think about it, Huk said, we always think death is making these things happen, but it's life really. Life happens and life is full of illnesses and accidents and everything else that happens to us. Death is close by *just in case*, but life makes things happen.

Death, Huk concluded, is actually really nice. He is not what we often make him out to be.

Did Duck think so? Tuk asked.

Yes, Huk replied. Duck slowly started to warm up to Death and even suggested they go to the pond together. Death didn't like the pond much. He didn't like the damp and cold, so once they returned from spending time at the pond, Duck offered to warm him a little and she spread herself over Death's cold body. No one had offered to warm Death up before.

This is a nice tale, Tuk thought. It puts Death in a friendly light. And that is truly reassuring and a reason we might not have to fear him so much.

When Duck and Death woke the next morning, Duck was very happy to be alive. For fun, she poked Death in the ribs, saying, I'm not dead.

That takes nerve, Tuk said, being able to joke around with Death.

Then Duck started to ask Death some questions, Huk continued. Some ducks say, Duck began, that you become an angel looking over the earth, and some ducks say that deep in the earth there is a place where you'll be roasted if you haven't been a good duck. Death responded by simply saying, You ducks come up with some amazing stories, but who knows?

Then Death asked, What shall we do today?

They decided not to go to the pond again but to climb a tree instead.

Duck wondered aloud what it would be like if she were dead. The pond would be alone, she said, alone without me.

Death finished the thought, saying, The pond will be gone too — at least for you.

That made Duck feel uncomfortable.

I would feel uncomfortable, too, said Tuk, and a little scared. The idea that nothing will be there anymore — at least for me — gives me the shivers. How can there be nothing left at all, all of a sudden? I know things will continue to *exist* without me, but how can I exist without anything around me? This is very confusing. I don't like it.

That's the mystery of death, Huk said, and the mystery of life too, actually.

Tuk was not satisfied and continued to feel uneasy about this whole thing. Wanting a distraction from these unsettling thoughts, Tuk asked Huk to continue with the tale.

When summer was ending, Huk continued, Duck and Death went to the pond less regularly. They often sat together in the grass, saying little.

Then one day Duck felt a chill and was cold. Can you warm me a little? she asked Death.

When the snowflakes started to drift down, Death saw Duck was no longer breathing. She lay quite still.

Tears started to well up in Tuk's eyes.

Huk noticed Tuk's sadness and tried to console Tuk. Huk said, Death stroked Duck's feathers and then carried her to the great river. He put her in the water and laid the tulip on top of her still body. Then he gently nudged her on her way. For a long time, he watched her and thought to himself, But that's life.

Huk and Tuk briefly looked at each other and considered what Death had said.

Tuk broke the silence. You know, maybe we should cherish life more — I mean, *before* we die.

Life and death do go *together*, Huk said, but we usually don't notice Death until we are ready to die.

Then Huk continued, I heard this story from the author of *our* stories. She says that before we came into this world, we were asked if we really wanted to live life on earth. Of course, we quickly replied, yes, of course. But then the follow-up question came, Even if it means that you will have to die? Not thinking twice, we replied again, Of course, yes! So here we are, so eager to live life on earth that we didn't pay much attention to the second half of the bargain — that we would have to die one day. And so, when we walk around like Duck, not assuming anything and finally noticing Death is close by, we are scared stiff, as we remember the bargain we signed on to.

That's an interesting idea, Huk, Tuk said. That may explain why we don't really pay attention to death. We simply forget death is part of life.

When we had our tails, Tuk continued, we were connected to life *and* death. We were connected to everything around us, and, remembering that death is always close by — all the time — we cherished things more.

Are you saying, Huk said, that when we lost our tails, we also lost our connection to death and thought death was not something to take seriously? That it was something we had control over?

Until we find out, Tuk said, that we have no control over death whatsoever.

Huk and Tuk were quiet for a while and marveled at the sunset — a sunset that, they both thought, was even more beautiful after this tale about Duck and Death and the tulip. It was peaceful and it made them feel that the world with all its woes and worries around things that were out of their control was also a place where they could feel at ease and that they could call home.

by Roger Gutierrez

How to Rejoice in What Is Beyond Our Control

— *Bear and Wolf* by Daniel Salmieri —

A few days later, Huk decided to go outside to see the night sky as it was slowly disappearing. A good time to visit Tuk, Huk thought, and watch the sunrise from Tuk's backyard.

As Huk walked over to Tuk's, Huk thought, It's interesting — if you think about it — that sunset and sunrise are equally beautiful.

When Huk arrived at Tuk's house, Tuk happily joined Huk in saying goodbye to the night sky and saying hello to the new day.

While they watched, Tuk said, I know another tale about two unlikely friends, sort of like Duck and Death.

What tale is that? Huk asked.

It's the tale of Bear and Wolf, said Tuk.

Let me get some hot tea, Tuk said, before I begin telling this tale. Hot tea goes well with sunrises, but also sunsets really.

Huk agreed, and Tuk headed inside to get some hibiscus tea for both of them.

When Tuk returned, Huk said what was on Huk's mind: Anyone can become friends. We only call friendships unlikely when we think of friends having to be similar, like only bears can be friends with bears and only wolves can be friends with wolves.

Even Duck and Death became friends, Huk added.

Tuk shuddered but agreed, You don't have to be the same to be friends. I think friendship is more about sharing, Tuk said, and Duck and Death did share in each other's company before Duck passed away.

Huk was quiet for a while and then said, smiling, And we are friends who love to share tales with each other — tales and tea. So do continue with your tale, Tuk, about Bear and Wolf.

One day, Tuk started, Bear was walking through a snowy forest when she spotted something through the glistening snow.

At the same time, Wolf was walking through the glistening snow and spotted something walking toward him.

As they got closer to each other, Bear saw a young wolf with a pointy snout, gray fur and a wet black nose.

Wolf saw the bear's round head, black fur and wet black nose.

Huk smiled. That's cute, Huk said. They both have a wet black nose.

Bear asked Wolf whether he was lost wandering through the forest on his own. And Wolf asked Bear whether she was lost wandering through the forest on her own.

I don't think they are lost, Huk thought. The forest is their home. You can't be lost in your home.

Both Bear and Wolf said that they loved feeling the cold air on their faces and hearing the quiet when it snows.

Can you hear the quiet? Huk wondered aloud.

Bear then told Wolf that she liked to walk through the forest and asked Wolf if he wanted to walk with her. Sure, Wolf replied. And off they went, walking through the quiet snowy world together.

It sounds a little like Frog and Toad when Frog left Toad a note on his door saying that he wanted to be alone. Remember when Toad finally found Frog sitting alone on the island and how Frog explained how he enjoyed being alone by himself but also enjoyed being alone together with Toad? asked Huk. Maybe Wolf and Bear enjoy being alone together, too.

Perhaps, said Tuk, they enjoy walking through this magical winter land alone together, smelling the wet bark of the trees, hearing the sound of snowflakes falling on their fur.

As they walked, Tuk continued, they suddenly spotted a snowy bird high up in the branches. And then Bird, from way up high, spotted Bear and Wolf down below.

Bird flew down from her branch to get a closer look of these two friends walking side by side through the peaceful and quiet snowy landscape.

As Bear and Wolf were walking alone together, they came upon a clearing in the forest. The clearing was a huge lake, now frozen and covered with snow. After they cleared away some of the snow, they could see fish floating. The fish were asleep deep in the water.

Then Bear told Wolf that she had to get back to her cave where she would sleep through the rest of

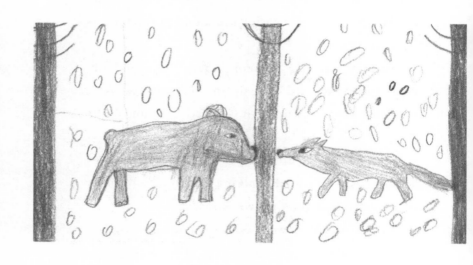

by Karlie Arreola

the winter until springtime when it was time to leave the den.

Then Wolf told Bear that he too had to leave and get back to his wolf pack.

They had loved being in each other's company and now they went their separate ways.

I really liked walking with you, said Bear.

I really liked walking with you, said Wolf. I hope we'll meet again.

They parted ways.

They spent the rest of the winter with their families until spring arrived. The snow had melted. The birds sang in the treetops. The forest burst with life.

And when Bear was walking through the lush green forest, she suddenly saw something through the green grass. It was Wolf.

And once again, Bear and Wolf took off together.

By the time Tuk had finished this tale, the sun was up and the friends had finished their tea.

Let's take a walk together like Bear and Wolf did, said Huk, and enjoy this incredible place we call home.

by Nevaeh Hernandez

Tuk agreed and said, Isn't it interesting to think — referring to the tale of Duck, Death and the tulip — that death is not the end of life, but perhaps the other way around, that life continues even after death, sort of how spring follows winter all over again? That's what I like about this tale, because after the cold winter, spring comes back and everything is full of life once again.

And that's life, Huk said with a big smile.

Tuk agreed, That's life.

by Roger Gutierrez

References

Epigraph

Robert S. Pirsig. *Lila: An Inquiry into Morals.* New York: Bantam Books, 1991, 322–23.

Chapter 1

Brooks, David. "Let's Have a Better Culture War." *The New York Times*, June 7, 2016.

Buber, Martin. *I and Thou.* Translated by Ronald Gregor Smith. New York: Charles Scribner's Sons, 1958.

Friedman, Maurice. *Martin Buber: The Life of Dialogue.* Chicago: The University of Chicago Press, 1976.

Watts, Alan. "Zen Bones." *Eastern Wisdom Collection.* Lecture available at www.alanwatts.org/audio/

Zen Bones: https://youtu.be/we_Cv2v8P4M

Zen Tales: https://youtu.be/54mkP1DJLDs

Chapter 2

Fingarette, Herbert. *Self-Deception*. New York: Humanities Press, 1969.

Lionni, Leo. *Alexander and the Wind-Up Mouse*. New York: Dragonfly Books, 1969.

———. *Fish Is Fish*. New York: Dragonfly Books, 1970.

———. *It's Mine*. New York: Dragonfly Books, 1985.

Lobel, Arnold. "The Club," in *Grasshopper on the Road*. New York: Harper & Row, Publishers, 1978.

———. "Cookies," in *Frog and Toad Together*. New York: Harper & Row, Publishers, 1972.

———. "The Voyage," in *Grasshopper on the Road*. New York: Harper & Row, Publishers, 1978.

Chapter 3

Lionni, Leo. *Cornelius*. New York: Dragonfly Books, 1983.

———. *Frederick*. New York: Dragonfly Books, 1967.

———. *Geraldine, the Music Mouse*. New York: Dragonfly Books, 1979.

———. *Matthew's Dream*. New York: Dragonfly Books, 1991.

———. *Tillie and the Wall*. New York: Dragonfly Books, 1989.

Lobel, Arnold. "The Dream" in *Frog and Toad Together*. New York: Harper & Row Publishers, 1972.

Chapter 4

Lionni, Leo. *Tico and the Golden Wings*. New York: Dragonfly Books, 1964.

Lobel, Arnold. "Always" in *Grasshopper on the Road*. New York: Harper & Row Publishers, 1978.

———. "Alone," in *Days with Frog and Toad*. New York: HarperCollins Publishers, 1979.

Silverstein, Shel. *The Giving Tree*. New York: HarperCollins Publishers, 1964.

———. *The Missing Piece*. New York: HarperCollins Publishers, 1976.

Steig, William. *Doctor De Soto*. New York: Farrar, Straus and Giroux, 1982.

Chapter 5

Erlbruch, Wolf. *Duck, Death and the Tulip*. Trans. Catherine Chidgey. New Zealand: English Translation Gecko Press, 2008.

Lobel, Arnold. "Dragons and Giants," in *Frog and Toad Together*. New York: HarperCollins Publishers, 1971.

———. "The Garden," in *Frog and Toad Together*. New York: HarperCollins Publishers, 1971.

———. "A New House," in *Grasshopper on the Road*. New York: HarperCollins Publishers, 1978.

Salmieri, Daniel. *Bear and Wolf*. New York: Enchanted Lion Books, 2018.

Acknowledgements

I would like to acknowledge the students at El Toyon Elementary School in San Diego, California. For three years prior to the COVID-19 pandemic, I led in-person classes in philosophy at El Toyon with students in first, second and third grade. During that time, I worked with teachers Yen Dang, Silvia Toledo, Patricia Carrillo, Pat Duran and Elizabeth McEvoy. I am thankful to these teachers for their dedication to doing philosophy with their students and encouraging them to think for themselves. Each class began with a picture book reading, which was followed by time for the students to think about the questions that came up for them and to then discuss these questions in small groups. Finally, I invited everyone to write down their thoughts about the story and to draw pictures.

During the COVID-19 lockdowns and restrictions, I continued working on the series with Patricia Carrillo and Yen Dang. When I couldn't be present in the classroom, these teachers would read the stories aloud and ask the children to explore the important questions they brought up. I am very grateful that we were able to continue the Huk and Tuk series in spite of the additional pressure the teachers and parents had to cope with during the pandemic. Thank you to all the students whose beautiful illustrations I've used in this series and to the parents who gave their permission to use them.

I also want to thank Blair Thornley, whose illustrations for *Why We Are in Need of Tails* so perfectly reflect the playful and whimsical nature of the story.

Once again, I am grateful for the feedback from my friend and colleague Claartje van Sijl, and, of course, from Mr. Lizzard. I also want to thank my auntie Martine Hellendoorn-Metzenheim, who suggested I combine all the books into one. Thanks as well to Becca Yuré, a former student of mine, for her wonderful audio recording of the story "Why We Are in Need of Making Choices with Our Eyes Wide

Open" and for writing the foreword for this book. I look forward to her reading of the entire collection.

Finally, thank you to Iguana Books: to its founder and director, Greg Ioannou, and former publisher, Meghan Behse, who both got Huk and Tuk into print in the first place; to its current publisher, Cheryl Hawley, who has pulled all the stories into a wonderful collection; to Toby Keymer for his meticulous proofreading eye; and to Holly Warren for doing the infinite editing dance with me, helping me on my writing journey to bring Huk and Tuk to life.

Maria daVenza Tillmanns was raised in the Netherlands and the United States and has moved across the Atlantic multiple times in the pursuit of the study and practice of philosophy. Maria developed a way of thinking — a philosophical way of thinking, as she later learned — that helped her navigate the bilingual and multicultural world she grew up in. She learned how to hold the tension between disparate ways of thinking and of being in the world.

In 1980, Maria attended Dr. Matthew Lipman's workshop on philosophy for children and later wrote her dissertation on philosophical counseling and teaching under the direction of Martin Buber scholar Dr. Maurice Friedman. For 15 years she worked at the University of California, San Diego, as a lecturer and as a union representative for lecturers and librarians.

Between 2017 and 2020, she taught a Philosophy with Children program in partnership with UCSD at El Toyon Elementary School, an underserved school in San Diego. For many years, she has headed two philosophical practice discussion groups, one in the United States and one that spans the globe. She has published in a number of international journals and professional magazines. For Maria, philosophy is an art form, one that has helped her navigate the world in all its complexity, and she enjoys painting with ideas. She now resides in San Diego with Mr. Lizzard and takes great joy in exploring the world with her companions Huk and Tuk.

Becca Yuré, PhD, BCBA, LBA, first met Professor Maria daVenza Tillmanns as her student at University of California San Diego. DaVenza Tillmanns stepped into the role of mentor by encouraging Yuré to think in new ways and supporting her learning and research endeavors. Yuré is a singer-songwriter and playwright, working to create accessible theater in New York City. Additionally, she works with children and their families supporting behavioral challenges and educates students in their masters and doctoral programs in this same field. Yuré is delighted to offer her voice to the *From Tails to Tales* stories in the forthcoming audiobooks.

Blair Thornley is an award-winning illustrator living in San Diego and Truro, Cape Cod. Among her extensive client list are *The New York Times*, *Boston Globe*, *Washington Post*, *Los Angeles Times*, *Vogue*, *Vanity Fair*, Herman Miller, and Neiman Marcus. She created the cover illustrations for a reprinted series of Peter De Vries's books and was a contributor to the recently published *Collected Fables* by James Thurber. Thornley's work is shown regularly at Harmon Gallery in Wellfleet, Massachusetts, and has been exhibited at Judy Saslow Gallery in Chicago, Pasadena Museum of California Art and at the Society of Illustrators in New York.

Exploring How the Huk and Tuk Series Is an Invitation to Dialogue

Maria daVenza Tillmanns, PhD

Abstract NAACI Conference in
Queretaro, Mexico

July 20 – 23, 2023

What makes Philosophy philosophical is that it asks questions about a world infinitely larger than ourselves. That has interesting implications, because we're not just asking questions that we can find an answer to, but about questions we cannot possibly answer; questions of not-knowing. For most, this level of uncertainty is unlivable. But, it is precisely this level of not-knowing that gives us the room to reflect. One cannot reflect on a closed system. A closed system with a final answer inhibits the questioning process. There is also a part of ourselves that is beyond our grasp of knowing and thereby creates the space to self-reflect. Philosophy creates the space necessary to pursue truth wherever it leads, as opposed to finding truth. Certainly, we have found truths in the sciences and truths about the human condition in the humanities. But these truths function as leads to ever-larger contexts of inquiry. Philosophy is the art of questioning and finds creative ways to ask the next question. Not all that different from a detective who always asks the next possible, even improbable question to create a bigger picture of what may have happened. The ancient Greek tradition of practicing parrhesia is in fact the tradition of not stopping at anything, even if it means questioning authority and those in power. This can be very daunting and it takes enormous courage to take the act of questioning that far. In fact, journalists nowadays around the world face death threats and death by asking questions that expose the practices of those in power. Parrhesia can also be practiced vis-à-vis the self. It involves relentless and rigorous self-questioning or self-critical questioning. The objective is not to find a final answer; it is the process of questioning itself that can lead us to far deeper ways of understanding. Understanding in contrast to knowledge can hold the tension between dichotomous viewpoints in a way that knowledge cannot. Knowledge teaches us that there can be either particles or waves, and not both. But by expanding our view to incorporate these dichotomous views gives us a deeper understanding of the world we live in. We have to incorporate many other factors as well, such as the role of the observer to get a broader view of this reality we are trying to understand. At the heart of the art of questioning is the notion of aporia, the ancient Greek notion of puzzlement and wonderment. But this notion of puzzlement is not non-committal. I have to be capable of putting one's beliefs and truths on the line for the sake of developing a deeper understanding. In the process, one discovers one's touchstones of reality, meaning those values underlining my beliefs and truths. These touchstones, however, are not cut in stone and can change as a result of developing a deeper understanding. Huk and Tuk, the main characters in the *From Tails to Tales* book series, model how to question the world and oneself freely. Huk and Tuk enjoy discussing picture book tales together and invite us into the dialogue as well. In the process we learn to not only reflect on the questions raised in these tales, but to self-reflect. What do I think and why? This exercise in self-reflection helps to develop self-knowledge — and getting to know oneself. Self-reflection is self-examination and a process that requires the courage to question one's self and with it that which gives the self its identity. To put one's identity on the line for the sake of developing a deeper understanding is not easily learned. We tend to respond reactively when we feel our identity is questioned and learning how to respond instead of react does not come easy. But to start this process with children when their beliefs are not yet cut in stone allows them to remain flexible thinkers as they grow up and cope with the uncertainty of ever-deeper questions. In fact, this type of questioning keeps their curiosity alive, which is otherwise often deadened with what we now call knowledge.

How to do 'Jazzy Philosophy': An Interview with Maria daVenza Tillmanns

Nathan Eckstrand, Maria daVenza Tillmanns
May 7, 2020

Maria daVenza Tillmanns does philosophy with children in an underserved school in San Diego. She says of her work, "Doing philosophy with young children is like painting with ideas, giving us a fuller and richer sense of their world. Philosophy is no longer grey, but bursting with color." This interview focuses on her most recent work, Why We Are in Need of Tails *(which was illustrated by the award-winning Blair Thornley). The book discusses how to build meaningful relationships.*

What is *Why We Are in Need of Tails* about? Why did you decide to write it?

The story is about the need to reconnect to others, the world around us, and ourselves. We have become too susceptible to empty rhetoric and others telling us what to think and do. The influence of advertising is overwhelming in ways we might not even be aware of. Increasingly, we have more reasons to distrust rather than trust each other. And if we trust, it often takes on the form of blind trust. We want to have blind trust and become cynical if we feel betrayed. How can we learn to trust again but with our eyes wide open instead of closed? How can we feel we belong to the world trustingly yet wisely? Huk and Tuk show how we can find ways to reconnect and develop meaningful relationships. Relationships we can build on in a constructive and creative way, open to change and integrating the wonders of being alive.

I had been writing articles based on my work doing philosophy with children in an underserved school in San Diego, when out of the blue, this whimsical story emerged, as if to take a break from all the heady stuff. This short story presents philosophical ideas in a playful, uncomplicated way. It is my way of painting with ideas, and an invitation for others to do the same. Philosophy is about life and cannot be purely theoretical, which it became when it became an ivory tower discipline.

Apart from Nietzsche being a fascinating philosopher, he is also a literary genius. His writing is inspirational, it's provocative and puzzling; it makes you think and rethink. He has tremendous insight into the human condition and human psychology. This insight is best conveyed through creative writing. It develops a deeper understanding. It is similar to zen koans which by creating doubt and perplexity force you to think at deeper levels in order to create a sense of aha! Understanding exists on a level that goes beyond knowing. My hope is that more philosophers will engage in philosophizing on paper. There really is no method to this kind of writing. Just as in art, artists develop their own style. And philosophers should also be able to develop their own style of philosophizing.

Your book is categorized as fiction. While philosophers (Sartre, Kierkegaard) have written fiction in the past as a way to convey philosophical ideas, it is rarely used. What led you to choose it?

I think fiction is more accessible to people of all walks of life and can be more fun to read. My short story is meant as a picture book for adults and young adults. And as in the case of picture books although meant for children — I am thinking of authors such as Arnold Lobel and Leo Leonni — picture books are metaphorical and can be interpreted and understood in many ways by all ages. They are a great resource for engaging in dialogue. I plan to write a next picture book with Blair Thornley in which I will give a short summary of one of Lobel's or Leonni's stories and have the characters Huk and Tuk discuss them in a way to promote philosophical dialogue. I hope this would give parents and teachers new ways of discussing complex life issues such as what it means to be brave, or why is being different considered with apprehension and distrust?

I like to think of my style of writing as jazzy philosophy, in that it is improvisational. As in jazz there are themes running across the story, but these themes are improvised on. And I'm not quite sure myself what direction it will go in until I'm actually writing it. In this way, it has a way of writing itself. This is stark contrast to academic writing, which is research-based.

My writing has never been strictly academic, but still found enough interest among several academic journals and professional magazines to be published. My guess is because my writing is philosophical and not strictly academic. Philosophical issues focus on questions regarding the human condition, regarding reality, how we know things, morality. While many academics do focus on these topics as well, I rarely see anyone among my colleagues philosophizing on these topics and just giving a stab at what they think about these topics. The research is very impressive and certainly indicates their focus and interest in what they are writing about. But what do *they* think? How is climate change influencing their thinking? How does the present human condition worry them or not? Do trans people change their thinking about what it is to be a human being?

What is the audience for the book?

The book is mostly for adults and inviting them to play along with me while thinking about complex issues around the difference between knowing and understanding or between monologue and dialogue or what it means to truly listen to another person and being able to hear them the way they hear themselves. It's about polyphonic listening. It's about feeling at home in the world we are already a part of. So often people see the meaning of life originating in the afterlife or in reincarnation or in life being predetermined. The meaning of life, for me, comes from being alive. I'm amazed what it means to be alive and breathing, period. I don't need any other explanations to give meaning and value to this life. So often people, who are close to death, value life for its own sake. This story invites people to enjoy life for its own sake. To live a full life, a life rich in meaning, which really means taking little for granted. Sure, we need to take certain things for granted to get through the day, but we also seem to take much for granted by not questioning things more. Children question everything; they are curious about everything and bombard you with questions to engage you in this mysterious world. They are not necessarily looking for answers, as much as they want to explore the world with you. And children are quite alive. They live a life of curiosity and engagement. And so should we.

Explain the purpose of your "Philosophy with Children" program. How did your work with that program influence this book?

Doing philosophy with children showed me how entrenched children are in life, if not more so than most adults. It also shows me that they have deeply insightful ideas about people and the world they live in simply because they are alive. Life itself informs them of what matters in life. We may think of morality as learned but I strongly believe it is an aspect of being alive. Children not only have ideas about the world, but also have a knack for connecting the dots, so to speak, in a way many adults have lost. Children's imagination should be fostered not tamed. We become very knowledgeable about the world, but often at the expense of our deeper understanding of the world. Doing philosophy with children enables them to further develop their imagination and innate understanding of the world.

Why We are in Need of Tails aspires to our imaginary world and hopes to create deeper understanding and with it a greater sense of emotional intelligence. We have created a world where knowledge is often gained at the expense of emotional intelligence or spiritual intelligence. Intelligence requires deep thinking and deep questioning which starts with creative imagination.

Your bio on the publisher's website makes a notable claim, that philosophy for you is an "art form." Describe what you see as the aesthetics dimension of philosophy.

Philosophy as an art form is related to philosophy as a way of life. Just as artists develop their particular styles, people should also be free to develop their own thinking. Just as being an artist requires much practice and training, so does developing your thinking. But in school we are mostly taught not just what to think but also how to think rather than how to develop our own thinking. We advocate for independent thinking, but much of independent thinking amounts to conforming to the thinking we were taught in school, at universities, in the communities, country and culture we grew up in and end up making our own. When children try to branch out on their own, families and society at large often try to reel them back in. Eventually society "wins." Once settled into a steady job, money issues a level of conformity that washes out the thrill and excitement that inspired so many people during their younger years. Philosophy should be the discipline through which young people learn to develop their own thinking. Just as we have an art academy, we should have a philosophy academy. Because just as being an art historian does not an artist make, so does being a scholar in the history of philosophy not make a philosopher. The question here could be: what made Socrates a philosopher?

Your bio also makes clear that philosophy is a way of life, inasmuch as it helps to wrestle with complexity. What advice do you have for people interested in using philosophy in this way?

I think life lived demands that you connect and re-connect the dots constantly. Conformist behavior comes from connecting the dots once and then imposing that framework upon everything else. That does not work. When we live our lives that way, we end up in conflict with people who do not conform to our way of thinking. If our thinking lacks flexibility, it cannot accommodate and appreciate how others think. It will exclude them from their fixed mind-set. Novel thinkers end up crashing against their conformist thinking. When doing philosophy with children it is so refreshing to see how flexible they are in their thinking, how easily they can change their minds when they hear something a peer said that somehow makes more sense to them. We lose our ability to connect to people, when we end up seeing them only through the fixed lens we have created for ourselves to give us a sense of certainty and purpose. If we disagree with someone's thinking, it stifles our ability to relate and connect to him. Our inflexible thinking gets in the way. So we need to learn to constantly see things from different angles, to constantly look for the bigger picture, to constantly reconnect the dots of what matters to us. Philosophy should be about flexible thinking, the aerobics of thinking, if you will.

So with this short picture book story, I would like to invite others to philosophize using creative writing as a means to express their thoughts and ideas. Fictional writing or poetry lends itself well for letting thoughts wander as they wonder.

Reproduced with permission from the Blog of the APA (American Philosophical Association).